I0557277

PAST INJUSTICE

A Mystery

Leonard Dawson

Table of Contents

THE KIDNAPPING

When fifteen-year-old Sara Jennings stepped outside her friend's house on Friday Night October 21st,, the driver of a brown van with rust spreading along its rocker panels like a skin disease told the man in the passenger seat, "That's her. That's Jenning's daughter, Sara."

A woman and a girl stood in the open doorway talking to Sara. The men were too far away to hear the woman tell Sara, "Your mother doesn't want you walking home alone. She said for you to wait here, that she'll come pick you up."

Sara didn't mean to sound irritated. It just came out that way when she told her friend's mother, "I'll be home before she leaves."

Although Eastwood Avenue runs straight as an arrow for three blocks then curves gently to the right, Sara could almost see her house five blocks away. When she heard the opening music to her friend's favorite television show, Sara told her friend to go back inside so she wouldn't miss anything then left for home.

Half a block away Sara stopped to try out a hopscotch grid chalked on the sidewalk that was just barely visible in the light from a nearby streetlamp. Hopping through the squares brought back memories of a less troubled time, reminding Sara of how much her world had changed.

Sara refused to buy into her mother's paranoia. Her mother's world might be an ugly place, but Sara's wasn't because she had a new boyfriend, and she was certain the crazy, mixed-

3

up emotions she felt for him were true love.

It was just like her mother to be jealous of her happiness. Why else would she tell Sara the world was a dangerous place just when Sara had found so much happiness in it? So Sara ignored her mother's warnings. Besides, she'd be home in five minutes. What could happen in five minutes?

She stepped off the sidewalk to kick through a mound of leaves, easing her frustrations at the expense of the neighbor who'd raked them into a pile. She thought about the desire she saw in the boy's eyes the first time he'd seen her naked, her skin tingling under his gaze, a moment she would remember forever.

The driver of the van had a big-boned face. His jaw, covered with a dense growth of dark stubble except for a line of old scar tissue where his hair wouldn't grow, worked on a piece of gum. A large muscular man who made the full-sized van appear cramped, he tapped his fingers on the steering wheel as he watched Sara, the muscles in his forearms rippling like snakes under his skin.

As Jason Reed, the scrawny little man sitting in the passenger seat, watched the girl who was now less than two blocks away, his left foot tapped nervously on the floor of the van. Strands of oily hair crisscrossed the top of his head leaving bare spots that were peppered with angry-looking red pimples. A wispy suggestion of a beard did little to hide his weak chin or the scars of old blemishes around his mouth.

Jason shook his head, saying, "It ain't right," over and over in a voice barely above a whisper, as though he was telling himself a secret.

Dean swung his right arm in a big backward arc toward Jason. Although Jason ducked to avoid Dean's fist, it brushed his jaw. After that Jason cowered in his seat with his arms over his head.

Dean looked away from Sara long enough to reach over and stiff-arm Jason, slamming his head against the window. After telling Jason, "You really don't want to make me mad," he turned back around to watch the girl.

Sara was walking through a neighborhood of small working-class houses, each of them with a small patch of grass in front. Most of them had bushes next to the house and a tree or two. A few of them had late-blooming flowers in flowerbeds by the front door. Conscientious young parents who had moved into the area to be near the local school so their kids could walk to class, kept the neighborhood looking tidy.

Sara spotted the van up ahead, about a block from her house, and although it looked out of place in her neighborhood, she dismissed it because she didn't want to come back from the fantasy rendezvous with her new love that was playing out in her head. She shut the world out as her lover's hand slid ever so slowly up her leg, as gently as the breath from a whisper. She didn't notice the pungent odor of the decaying wet leaves in the gutter, or feel the coolness of the night air, or feel her clothes, buffeted by the wind, fluttering against her skin.

Moments later she was startled by the throbbing of the van's engine. Annoyed that it had intruded on her thoughts again, she paused for a moment to look at it. The van that had just looked out-of-place moments before now looked ominous.

She pushed it out of her happy thoughts, but an uneasiness had settled in her mind and it stayed with her, fading in and out just beneath her consciousness, the way her shadow appeared behind her out of the blackness, slipped past her as she walked under a streetlight then faded back into the blackness beyond the reach of the light.

We are who we are in spite of ourselves, and the girl Sara had become could no more accept the evil closing in on her than the leaves blowing down the street past her could go back where they came from.

Glancing at Dean then at the girl, Jason said, "I can't do this."

Dean grabbed Jason's arm and twisted it toward the front of the van, causing Jason's forehead to slam into the metal dashboard with a dull thump. "Do like I told you, Reed, or I'll snap your arm like a chicken bone."

5

Jason twisted around in his seat to relieve the pressure on his arm. "Okay, okay. Let go."

Dean let it go. Jason leaned away from him, cowering against his door. Dean reached over and grabbed Jason's neck, squeezing it until Jason's face turned deep red. "I waited sixteen years for this, Reed. I will kill you if you screw it up."

Then he grabbed Jason's shirt and yanked him out of his seat toward the back of the van, saying, "Now get out there."

Jason pulled a ski mask out of his coat pocket as he stepped down out of the van. He didn't put it on yet because Dean had told him to wait until he got close to the girl so no one else would see him wearing it. The van pulled away from the curb. Jason didn't want any part of kidnapping the girl, but he had no doubt, that if he backed out now Dean would torture him just for the fun of it, then kill him in some unimaginably horrible way. Jason walked toward Sara.

Sara had asked her mother if she could go to a rock concert a week from Saturday because the boy she liked was going. She had ignored the little voice in her head that told her not to mention the boy, but Sara was so excited about seeing him she couldn't possibly hold it in. Her mother, who had heard bad things about the boy, told Sara he was trouble, and that she wasn't allowed to see him.

Her mother was right, the boy would be trouble for Sara, but not in the way her mother expected. Because Sara was preoccupied with figuring out a way to get to the concert to see him, she wasn't paying attention as Jason and the van closed in on her.

As he drove toward Sara, Dean said to no one in particular, "It's payback time, bitch."

Ten feet past Sara he swung the van across the street toward the opposite curb to start a "K" turn. After backing up then pulling forward again he was behind her. He drove ahead slowly, gradually closing the distance between them as he watched Jason's shadowy figure angling across the street toward Sara.

As he crossed the street, Jason passed from the shadow of an old oak with a dense canopy of leaves into the light of a streetlamp. So to Sara, he appeared suddenly, out of nowhere, like a phantom. Although the sight of him had startled her, her attention was drawn back to the deep throbbing sound of the van as it came up behind her.

Stopping to glance back, she saw that the van wasn't more than a car length behind her. Something wasn't right. It was going too slowly. When her mind finally realized the danger, Sara looked around for help but saw no one. Her familiar surroundings were now as unfamiliar as a street corner in a foreign country. She shook her head, as though by denying her new reality she could alter it.

Startled again, this time by the sound of footsteps behind her, she turned around and saw Jason wearing a mask. Fear and confusion caused her to hesitate. Indecision became paralysis. Her adrenaline surged. Her pulse raced. It left her feeling dizzy and nauseous, breathing hard but short of breath. She felt her heart pounding in her chest and heard it thundering in her ears.

She heard a car door close behind her. She looked back over her shoulder. A big man wearing a ski mask was coming toward her. She heard footfalls behind her. It was the little man. He was closing in too. Instinct took over. She ran for the nearest house.

Stepping sideways, Dean blocked her path. Sara collided with him, twisting to avoid his grasp. Slipping a hand around her torso, Dean lifted her off the ground. His arm felt like a clamp. She managed to get out the start of a scream before his other hand covered her mouth. She struggled. He carried her to the van, stepping up into the back of it with her as though she was a little girl's doll.

By the time Reed climbed into the van, Sara was kicking and punching wildly. "Duct tape her mouth, Reed, before she bites me."

Reed told Dean to do it himself then pulled Dean's ski mask up. Sara's eyes connected with Dean's, just for a moment before Dean pulled the mask back down, but it had been enough. She'd be able to identify him later. Dean punched Sara in the gut then dropped her on the floor. She curled up and gasped for air. Jason was backing up. Dean spun around but couldn't reach him. Dean lunged for him. Jason jumped out of the van. Dean saw him disappear into the night. Dean knelt down to tape Sara's mouth.

Still struggling for breath, Sara rolled over onto her stomach and tried to get a leg under her. Dean put his knee in her back to hold her down while he put tape on her wrists, and ankles. He walked back to where he'd grabbed Sara to get the purse she'd dropped. Thirty minutes later, Dean parked the van near a cabin in a densely wooded valley.

He pulled Sara out of the van and dragged her to the door, holding onto her squirming body with one arm while he pounded on the door. Dean shoved Jack, the man who'd answered the door wearing a mask, out of the way, carrying Sara inside.

Jack asked Dean, "Where's Reed?"

Pushing past him, Dean said simply, "Change of plans," then carried Sara down a hallway to one of the bedrooms where Jack helped Dean tie her to the bed and secure a hood over her head.

When they were back in the kitchen, Dean tore a page out of the phone book. He drew a rough map showing how to get to Sara's house. Then he nodded toward the back door. Jack followed him outside, closing the door behind them. Dean stepped closer to Jack, getting within inches of his face. Unable to stand the reek of Dean's cheap cologne, and the threat of his nearness, Jack turned his face away. He and girls at the Tender Loin had joked about it when Dean was at the club, before he went to prison. Dean had been known for the nasty stuff. Thinking about it gave Jack an idea.

Dean slapped the map against Jack's chest. "This is how you get to the kid's place. I'll call you when it's time to take her home. You get her there ASAP, no screwing around and no wasting time. You hear me?"

Jack nodded his head. Sara was a good-looking kid, but Dean was crazy. He had no doubt that Dean would fillet him. Hell, he knew Dean had done worse things.

Dean started to walk toward his van. Stopping halfway there, he spun around and glared at Jack. "If you so much as touch that girl I'll fillet you before I kill you.

Jack watched the van disappear in the trees before he went back inside. On his way to Dean's room, Jack thought about how satisfying it would be to rape Sara and have Dean go to prison for it. And with Reed out of the picture it was possible. Jack applied a liberal dose of Dean's cologne before going to the bedroom.

Driving back to Eastwood Avenue, past the spot where he'd kidnapped Sara, Dean pulled into the driveway at Sara's house. Driving to the end of it, near the back of the house, he parked the van where it wouldn't be seen by nosy neighbors. Then he walked around to the front of the house, grinning as he knocked on the front door, because even though the payback would only last a few minutes, he'd waited years to savor it.

The woman who answered the door didn't say anything, just blinked her eyes several times, as though the sight of Dean had confused her. A moment later the woman tilted her head and frowned. Dean knew then that a piece of her past had appeared to her, floating just beyond her grasp. When Dean saw the color drain from her face and heard a sudden intake of breath, he knew she'd remembered him. He shoved her so hard she stumbled backwards into the house and fell on the floor. He heard a thud when her head bounced on the glossy wood.

Dean tossed Sara's purse at her. The woman sat up where she'd fallen and picked up the purse. The way she studied it, it might have been something foreign. She looked inside it then looked at Dean then looked at the purse again. The purse dropped first, then her jaw, as she put her hands over her mouth and uttered Sara's name barely audibly.

Kneeling down next to her, Dean grabbed her hair. He pulled her head back hard enough to make her wince. With his lips so close to her ear that she would feel the heat of his breath, he whispered, "I had sixteen years to think about tonight. That's a very long time."

"I'll do anything you want if you'll leave Sara out of this."

Dean pushed her down on the floor. "It'll be like old times."

THE MURDER

On Friday Night October 21st, a dark blue Lincoln Mark IV entered a quiet residential neighborhood. Urbanization had leapfrogged right over the area, leaving an enclave of stately old homes with large lawns, ornamental fences, and mature plantings. The homeowners believed that their refuge would forever remain safe from the relentless creep of urban crime. Of course, they were wrong. Crime doesn't play leapfrog.

The driver pulled into the parking lot of the St. James Catholic Church, parking across from twenty-two Congress Street, a big, white, austere-looking Federal house with a tall ornamental iron fence enclosing the entire yard. Although lights were on in the back of the house, the windows in the rest of the house were all dark.

After looking at his watch, he checked to be sure there were no cars or pedestrians coming before pulling his hood over his head. He put gloves on then got out of the car with a gym bag. Walking at a leisurely pace with his head down, as though he was a local resident returning home late, he walked to the corner of Whig and Congress streets, turning right on Whig. Half a block later he turned right into an alley that would take him behind the houses on Congress Street.

He stopped behind number twenty-two to kneel down with his bag. He took out a large folding knife, which he put in his left pocket. Then, taking out a baseball, he lobbed it high over the fence. It hit the ground with a thud. He listened for a

11

dog barking but heard only the faint sound of traffic passing by several blocks away on the four-lane.

After backing up from the fence about ten feet, he ran toward it at an angle. With his left hand on the top of the fence as he jumped, he cleared it with ease. He walked behind the garage located twenty feet behind the house, a throwback from the era of detached garages.

From the corner of the garage he could see that the curtains in the back room were closed, and knew a television was on in there from the way light flashed on them. Walking to the back wall of the house, he crouched behind an overgrown yew bush near the side door then checked the area. The house next door was dark except for a weak porch light and the street was empty.

He took the keys out. Standing so that someone at the neighbor's house could only see his back, but angled a little, so someone on the street wouldn't be able to see his full profile and later identify him, he pulled his hood off.

After stepping up to the side door he took the knife out and opened it then rang the bell. He tensed when he heard the latch. He'd only have a split second, no room for error. The door had only opened a crack when he forced it back, shoving as hard as he could, knocking the woman inside off balance.

Kicking the door closed, he lunged for the woman. She hesitated; a moment lost before she tried to run. He grabbed her from behind. She twisted. He placed his left hand over her mouth, pulled her head back, ending her life with the knife.

When her struggling stopped he dropped her on the floor like a discarded doll. She came to rest leaning against the wall with her legs splayed out and her chin slumped on her chest, as though she was watching the spreading stain on her flower-print dress.

He used her dress to wipe the blood off of his knife. Seeing her like that was a relief, but he didn't have time to enjoy his handiwork. He opened the door enough to see outside. With no one in sight he slipped out the way he came.

CHAPTER I

My name is Andrew Lee. I have small law firm in Ithaca, New York. I've practiced law as a public defender for more years than I care to count. But I had never worked on what I considered a high-profile case, not until Sheila Eams was killed at her boyfriend's house. When the police arrested her husband, Arthur Eams, for her murder, he hired me to defend him.

As luck would have it, the next day I was appointed defense counsel for Ronald Dean, who had been charged with kidnapping Sara Jennings, a sixteen-year-old girl, and raping her mother. Both Sara and her mother had identified Dean in a lineup.

Since guilty verdicts for the kidnapping and the rape were a near certainty, my job was getting Dean a reduced sentence, if that was even possible. I wondered how well I'd sleep knowing I'd be putting Dean back on the street sooner. And I wondered how my wife and my friends would feel about me defending Dean, even if it hadn't been my choice.

Dean was arraigned Monday October 24th. I met him for the first time the next morning. He was to be questioned at the county jail at 9:00 AM. I was to meet him there at 8:30. The jail was located north of town at the top of East Hill.

Route 13 south out of Ithaca doesn't require you to climb a hill. All of the other routes out of Ithaca do. You see "steep downhill grade" or "test your brakes" warning signs on several of the hills leading into Ithaca. Route 96B into Ithaca from the south runs past Ithaca College. It has a required turnout for trucks, where they must come to a stop before descending the hill. Of course, without the hills Ithaca wouldn't have over a hundred waterfalls and dozens of scenic gorges.

From the highway, which climbs up East Hill in a long sweeping curve, I saw cotton-like whitecaps drifting across Cayuga Lake. Several sailboats leaned hard against the wind, their owners taking advantage of the recent warm spell to extend their summer. From Cayuga Lake, avid sailors can take their boats through a series of locks to Lake Ontario, then up the St Lawrence Seaway to the Atlantic Ocean. I have a friend who does that every year. I should put more effort into cultivating his friendship.

My four-cylinder compact labored up the hill, the pitch of the engine jumping up an octave as the automatic transmission downshifted to get more power. The pitch dropped an octave when the transmission shifted into a lower gear after reaching cruising speed. That process repeated itself all the way up the hill. My car's unsettling struggle was a fitting prelude to my meeting with Dean.

The design of the new jail clashed jarringly with the classic architecture of the government buildings in downtown Ithaca, buildings whose designs symbolized our admiration for classical Greek culture. I wondered what kind of values had inspired the architect of the new jail, because everything about the one-story, concrete-block building was industrial, colorless, and uninviting. And the token clumps of shrubs and saplings planted around the place did little to improve the bleak atmosphere.

At the jail, one of the guards led me to a small room where Dean was waiting for me. He stood with his back to me looking outdoors through the bars on the only window. Chains hung from his wrists and ankles. I'm not a small guy, but Dean looked imposing, probably well over two hundred pounds and definitely over six feet.

The walls were unpainted cinder block; the floors, plain

gray linoleum The furniture consisted of two gray metal chairs, the padded seats patched with gray duct tape, and a gray table with paint worn down to the bare metal in places. Strikingly out of place in the new building, the furniture had obviously been brought from the old jail.

I told the guard to remove the chain connecting Dean's arm and leg cuffs.

He said, "I don't think that's a good idea, sir."

I insisted. I shouldn't have.

He removed the chain then said, "The handcuffs stay on," adding, "Watch yourself," before leaving the room.

When I told Dean, "I'm Andrew Lee," I didn't get a response. I tried again. "Like it or not, Dean, you need to talk to me."

He turned around. He wasn't at all what I had expected. There was nothing in his features that would make people wary of him. His nose and mouth were both well-defined and well-proportioned, and set in a lean face with a strong jaw-line. He was clean shaven and his brown hair was cut short. His jaw muscles flexed as he clenched his teeth.

He came toward me. When he was about three feet from me his head jerked suddenly to the right, as though something had surprised him. It threw me off, just for a split-second, but enough time for him to grab my arm and twist it behind me. He had moved so fast it was all over by the time I realized what was happening. I hadn't expected anything like that, not with the guard right outside.

I suppose he did it to prove that I wasn't safe from him, even when he was in jail, because a moment later he grinned at me then let me go, saying, "You're gonna get the DA to cut me a deal, and it had better be a good one."

I told him I'd do my best.

"Oh, you'll do better than that, Andy. You know how I know that?"

I shook my head.

"Because I can get to Mel, even from in here."

I warned him to stay away from my wife, but he just grinned at me. I pounded on the door. The guard came in. He put the chain between Dean's arm and leg cuffs back on before leading him to chair at the table. He hooked Dean's chains to a ring in the floor.

Dean's threat against Mel really had me rattled, the fact that he even knew her name had me spooked. It also bothered me that Dean had caught me off-guard so easily. Of late, I'd thought I was at the top of my game. But success is a bit like a rock in a river that you swim long and hard against the current to reach. Sitting on the rock, above the raging water, you feel safe so you linger there. But then one day when your guard is down the water sweeps you back into the river and you're swimming for the rock again. It appeared that getting back to the rock would be a real challenge this time.

Even though it wasn't hot that day, I felt sweat beading up on my face, felt its slimy wetness on my palms. I sat at the far end of the table from Dean. The last thing I wanted was to see someone I knew, but my friend, Detective Mike Walters, came in. One of the few people on the police force who had always been civil to me, a decent guy who had always cut me some slack, even though it was my job to free the scum they pulled off the street. I had no doubt that he'd taken some grief for being my friend.

Considering the demands of his job, Mike carried more weight around than he should have, although he was in better condition than his appearance suggested. But some thirty years on the job had taken their toll, leaving deep lines in a face that looked so ruddy I worried about his blood pressure.

The dense salt and pepper stubble on his chin contrasted with the thinning gray hair on his head, wispy remnants of the thick, wavy black hair he'd had back when I first met him. Large brown eyes looked out from beneath bushy eyebrows. His nose and mouth, and the shape of his face, all ill-defined and rough-looking, created a tough-guy persona that would be a plus in his profession.

Mike sat down across from me and nodded toward Dean.

"Humanity's trash is always blowing through this place, but this guy's different. People like him change you. We say we're not gonna let that happen, but one day you realize you're not the same person. You no longer believe that you can make a difference, and you don't remember when you lost that."

CHAPTER II

Dean's lips turned up just slightly at the corners when I looked at him, hinting at cruelty. His eyes, gray and dull, studied us with the intensity of a predator.

After Mike went through some formalities to document the interrogation session, he told Dean, "You would save us all a lot of trouble if you just told us what happened that night."

Before I had a chance to advise Dean about his answer he held up his hand, cutting me off. If Dean wanted to talk, all the better. Hell, if he rolled over and confessed, I'd buy Mike a drink to celebrate.

Of course, that's not the way it happened. Instead, Dean told Mike. "I got nothin' to say unless you've got a deal for me."

"No deal," Mike said. "We're going to put you away forever."

Dean shook his head. "Not for kidnapping, you're not."

"Yeah, pretend it wasn't you who raped Sara and her mother. See if that works."

Dean looked as though he'd been gut-punched. "You got nothing on me but the kidnapping."

"And yet we do," Mike said.

Dean slammed his fists on the table. "That's not possible."

"And yet it is."

Dean's jaw set. He squinted. "Maybe you can get me for doing the old lady, but not the kid. I didn't touch her."

Dean was convincing. Of course he would be, career felons

get plenty of chances to hone their acting skills.

Mike wasn't buying it. "Sara said it was you, Dean, and she's sixteen. You know as well as I do how that's going play with a jury."

Dean thrashed against the chains in a disturbing display of anger. When his storm subsided, he hung his head, but still insisted that he hadn't touched Sara.

A lot of the repeat criminals parading through the criminal justice system had burned out most of their gray cells, but that didn't seem to be the case with Dean. He definitely had some demons clambering around in his head, but he didn't come across as stupid. And he did seem genuinely surprised.

I asked Mike about the rape charges.

"The girl and her mother both said they were raped. The doctor found bruises on the girl that are consistent with that."

"But not on her mother?"

Dean's eyes scanned the room, as though he was looking for answers to questions Mike hadn't asked him. Once again he said, "I didn't touch her," repeating it several times, as if that would change anything.

Mike said to Dean, "You picked up Sara at eight o'clock. We know that because Sara's friend always watches "Growing Pains" and it had just started. Sara said you took her someplace in a van and that you raped her. Mrs. Jennings said you showed up at her place at around nine o'clock. She knew that because she had something in the oven and was watching the time. After you showed Mrs. Jennings Sara's purse, you told her you'd hurt Sara unless Mrs. Jennings did what you told her."

While Dean sat silently, shaking his head with his eyes closed, Mike told me, "Apparently Dean's accomplice pulled his mask off when they grabbed her. So Sara got a good look at him, not to mention a whiff of his cologne. She smelled the same cologne later when he raped her."

"Did I hear you right, Mike, that Sara ID'd Dean from the smell of his cologne?"

"Stuff's pretty foul, Andy. It'd be hard to mistake."

It occurred to me that I might persuade the jury to find Dean innocent if I suggested that someone else had been wearing his cologne. Of course, the thought of Dean being acquitted was intensely disturbing. Mel and I would have to leave town if he was acquitted. But I expected Francis to put Sara on the stand, and if she testified... Well juries have a lot of sympathy when it comes to kids.

Dean was still denying that he'd molested Sara when they led him away. I asked Mike how they'd found Sara.

He took a sip of his coffee then made a face and pushed his cup aside. "Dogs barking at Mrs. Jennings' neighbor's place got her attention. Dean had dumped Sara, bound and gagged, on the lawn outside her house."

I thanked Mike and asked him to say "hi" to his wife for me.

As I was going out the door Mike said, "I don't envy you, Andy. The press is gonna be all over this, and you're definitely on the wrong side of the fence this time."

I didn't envy me either. Before I left the jail, I used someone's phone to call Mel and ask her to meet me at Morey's Diner for a late breakfast. Morey's Diner was a throwback to those long narrow silver buildings that shine like a big chrome bumper from the fifties. Morey's was on the four-lane a little south of town near Buttermilk Falls, a deep, picturesque gorge carved out of shale deposits by a river the color of its name.

Morey had died years earlier, but his wife Dorris had kept the place open. She would start cooking in the morning when the birds began to stir, and would still be hard at work when the bars closed early the next morning. In years, she was seventy-something. In pounds, she wasn't much more than that.

Dorris had the deep raspy voice of a long-time smoker, her breath occasionally whistling through the gap left by a missing tooth. She did all of the cooking, and when the waitress was busy, she served what she cooked. At the end of the day, she wiped and scrubbed and mopped, and then got ready to do it all over again. Maybe it was her way of hanging onto the past.

Maybe she had to do it to get by.

The early breakfast crowd had already left by the time I got there. With only a few customers scattered about the dining room my entrance was too conspicuous to go unnoticed. Several of the patrons eyed me as I walked to the back of the room where Mel was waiting for me in a booth. She'd worn a plain white blouse with a small gold heart suspended from a single strand of thin gold chain that matched the color of her shoulder-length hair.

When I got here she was idly flipping through the song selections on the juke box controller on the wall over the table. Besides being my wife for many years, Mel has been a valuable assistant, providing me with insights into the personalities of my clients, because reading people was not one of my strong suits.

As I slid into the booth across from her she told me, "You don't look so good."

"I'm fine."

"Oh really, 'cause you have the look of someone whose dog just died."

Much as I didn't want to talk about it, I knew she wouldn't relent until I opened up. "I met my new client this morning."

"And?"

"And I've had better mornings."

It was about to get a lot worse.

CHAPTER III

Mel said, "Let me guess, Andy. You can't ask to have the case reassigned to someone else."

"That's right."

"You used to talk about making the world a better place. That's why you wanted to be a lawyer, remember?"

"I remember having this discussion before."

"Sorry, Andy, but I think the world's pretty much the same it was when you started down that road."

Dorris' only waitress, Brenda, I think, made it to our booth then. Brenda had a grating, scratchy, low voice that reminded me of Bluto, Popeye's rival for Olive Oyl. Brenda was much too matronly to be Olive Oyl.

She set two coffees and a pile of creamers down between us, spilling both of the coffees into their saucers. Drinking Dorris' coffee is something of an adventure, akin to drinking the water in Mexico. The waitress left without taking our orders. That would have to wait until the mood struck her.

Mel, bless her heart, remembered right where we'd left off. "You're always talking about doing something else, but you never do."

She was right. I often talked about switching from criminal law to some form of business law, but I hadn't done it yet. At some point, my striving to reach some vague level of accomplishment had morphed into treading water in a comfort zone. A big change sounds great until you have to shed all of the things that make you feel comfortable.

If life is like a river, then starting over is like walking down to the bank and leaping into the foaming white rapids, all the while hoping it's going to take you to a new place better than the one you left. And you think that maybe, just maybe, it's where you'll find the meaning that's been lacking in your life.

I told Mel that, even though my job wasn't what I'd hoped for, it did put food on the table. It didn't have the effect I'd hoped for.

She went on as though she hadn't heard me. "And don't talk to me about the justice system as though it's the manifestation of some lofty ideal, because it broke a long time ago."

I tried patting her hand but that was like pouring gas on a fire. She began talking louder, loud enough that people at the next table looked our way. "Your precious 'system' is based on outdated precedents. It's mired in technicalities. And it expends all of its energy perpetuating itself. Justice is a regular casualty of the justice system."

I had to admit there were days when I felt the same way, this being one of them, so I let it go.

With her lip quivering she said, "See how upset you've made me, Andy?"

Our waitress came back again. This time she stood sideways to us, leaning against the table and glaring down at me over her shoulder, her big beefy hands holding a little stub of a pencil over her order pad. She cleared her throat to let us know she was ready to take our orders.

Mel and I both ordered menu selection number one, two eggs with toast and home fries. The waitress wrote our orders on her pad slowly and carefully. At Dorris', you order by the numbers printed on the menu, and if you don't, the waitress makes a production out of looking up the number. The odd thing is that, when you order by the number on the menu, she yells the specifics of the order to Dorris without first looking it up. Apparently, she's just a real stickler for procedure. It doesn't bother me, but I feel sorry for her kids, assuming something highly unlikely happened and she actually had some.

Before she left our table, she yelled our orders to Dorris loud enough to be heard in the parking lot. Then she opened one of the menus on the table to look up the price, which I'm sure she knew because it's the special as well as the first selection on a one-page menu.

As Mel watched the waitress leave, she asked me, "So, what are you gonna do?"

"About what?"

"The Dean case, silly. Try to keep up, Andy."

"Dean wants me to cut a deal with the DA."

I think that took Mel by surprise because her gaze shifted from the waitress back to me. "He thinks he can get a deal after what he did to that girl?"

I couldn't believe she'd already heard what happened to Sara. "How'd you find out about that already?"

She seemed surprised that I was surprised. "It was in the paper, silly."

"That's not right, Mel. I'm his lawyer and I didn't know about it until this morning."

"He confessed, Andy. How could you not know that?"

"I don't know where the paper got its information, but he didn't confess to that."

"Yeah? What did he confess to?"

"I don't know, but so far, he's only been charged with assaulting the mother and kidnapping the girl. He's adamant that he didn't touch her."

"And you believe him?"

A movement on the periphery of my vision got my attention.

Mel tapped my arm. "Hey, I asked you a question."

Brenda, who, until then, had been standing by the cash register reading a newspaper, had for some reason taken a renewed interest in us. I told Mel that something was up.

"Yeah, you're losing your grip."

24

"What's that supposed to mean?"

"I'm disparaging your judgment, Andy."

"I chose you, didn't I?"

Mel was saying, "That was just a lucky guess," when the Brenda slammed a folded newspaper down on our table. It landed with a grainy picture of me staring back at me. The caption read, "Dean's Attorney, Andrew Lee." I felt as though I'd been gut punched, or maybe it was Dorris' coffee.

Brenda hovered over me, pointing at the picture like an angry parent, scolding me in that Bluto-like voice of hers. "That's you, ain't it?"

"Yeah, but it's not my good side."

"It says here you're defending that guy." She tapped on the picture impatiently then asked, "Is that true?"

I told her it was.

Mel said, "I don't believe this."

Brenda's first mistake was turning her back on Mel. Her second mistake was saying, "No decent man would do what you're doing," loud enough to be heard by everyone in the place.

Mel slammed her hand down on the table so hard it sounded like a gun shot. That got Brenda's attention, and before she had a chance to recover, Mel lit into her. "He didn't ask for the case. If you're angry about it, go complain to the judge who assigned it to him."

Brenda put her big meaty hands on her more than ample hips and glared back at Mel. "You're not getting served here."

As Brenda walked away Mel said, "Bitch," to her back.

Brenda spun around, taking big, John Wayne strides back toward Mel. I stepped out of the booth to cut her off before the two of them made contact.

The place was eerily silent except for the sound of Dorris' spatula and her sizzling grill. A diner full of angry customers might be unsettling, but standing between two angry women is beyond frightening.

Brenda blocked the aisle, challenging Mel to escalate the confrontation. I tossed a wad of bills on the table, more than enough to pay for the food we didn't eat and the service we didn't get. By that time, Mel was on her feet and looking every bit as mad as Brenda, so I grabbed Mel's arm, pulling her around behind me, hoping to defuse the situation.

I said, "Excuse us," to Brenda as forcefully as I could.

She stood her ground, glaring at us, for so long I began to think she wasn't going to let us leave. When she did finally step aside, I guided Mel around behind me, carefully staying between the two women.

We left with everyone's eyes upon us, like celebrities, but not the idolized type. When we reached the car Mel spun around. "This sucks, Andy. I like living here."

"It'll blow over."

"But it'll never be quite the same, will it? We won't even feel comfortable eating at our favorite diner."

"Maybe this would be a good time to go see Arthur Eams."

"Is that an invitation?"

"I want to know what you think of the guy."

That had the desired effect of calming her down, if only a little.

CHAPTER IV

By the time we left the diner the sky was threatening rain. It had turned a uniform, off-white color, like a sheet of light-gray paper. We took Mel's late-model Chevy Nova. She never liked riding in my car; she says it's shabby looking. We followed Court Street west over the canal past the old Ithaca train station then turned right, heading north on Taughannock Boulevard.

Someone had converted the defunct train station into a restaurant serving fine food in authentic railroad dining cars. Waiters record the customer's selections of entrees, sides, and desserts by punching holes in preprinted tickets they carry on metal loops, like the ones train conductors carried in the age of steam, punching holes to denote destinations.

I told Mel to slow down as we approached a boat storage facility. Pointing across the street at a nondescript commercial building, I told her to park next to the dark-blue Lincoln.

Mel asked me how I knew it was a Lincoln, a trap I stumbled into by telling her, "Because it looks like a Lincoln."

"Way to waste those brain cells, Andy."

As she pulled into the parking lot she remarked on the Lincoln. "It looks out of place here."

"That's the whole point of a status symbol, isn't it?"

After parking in front of the one-story metal-clad building and shutting the car off she put her hand on my arm to keep me from getting out of the car. "Tell me about this guy before we go in."

"He owns a big auto graveyard near Spencer. Apparently, there's big money in used car parts. He also does some repo work. And he owns a bunch of student apartments up in College Town."

Mel looked straight ahead. Something was obviously bothering her. "We're good people, aren't we, Andy?

"You know we are, Mel"

"I drive a middle class car. You drive a clunker"

I told her that the disparaging comment about my car was uncalled for.

She ignored me. "This guy's a slumlord, and God knows what else. And yet he drives an expensive new car."

"Yeah, but we have each other."

She looked at me and smiled. "Nice one, Hon."

"And don't envy him the car."

"Why not?"

"Note the roof."

"Noted. Now, tell me why I noted it."

"Because it's unusual, maybe the only one in the area, and a witness saw it at the murder scene."

"I never thought I'd say this, Andy, but I see your point. He'd be better off if he drove an old piece of junk like your car."

"You never thought you'd say which part? That you see my point? Or that he'd be better off driving drive an old piece of junk like mine?"

It got a smirk. She got out of the car. I led the way to the front door, holding it open for her in spite of the insult to my car. The glaring lack of decor and the industrial-gray color scheme of Arthur's reception room reminded me of where I'd met with Dean except that the front wall, including the door, was all windows, affording an unobstructed view of the boat storage warehouse across the street, and a yard full of pleasure boats, some of them nearly as big as our house.

A woman sat behind a large metal desk on the far side of the room typing something, her fingers moving so fast the clicking of her fingernails on the keys sounded like a hard-driving rain. Wearing a plain, light-blue blouse tailored like a man's shirt, with her brown hair tied up on her head in a swirl. She could have been a librarian, except that her blouse was unbuttoned enough to reveal a glimpse of her pink bra. It may have been accidental, but I didn't think so.

She neither looked at us, nor missed a beat on the keys. "What can I do for you?"

"I'm Andrew Lee, Arthur's lawyer. I'd like to talk with him."

I wasn't sure she'd heard me because the typing continued unabated, so I added, "Now would be a good time."

I looked around the room while I waited for some kind of acknowledgment. The only furniture in the room, other than the receptionist's desk, was a group of cheap-looking metal chairs arranged around a coffee table near the front windows. All of them had plastic seats, no two of which were the same color.

The only door besides the door we came in, was behind the woman's desk, so it had to be the door to Arthur's office. Because he was a landlord and repo agent, I suspected Arthur wasn't eager to see most of the people who came to his office. His secretary had no doubt been posted in front of his door to guard it.

I checked the phone on her desk. One of the status lights was lit. Arthur was probably on the phone. It explained why she'd kept us waiting. When I saw the phone light go off I cleared my throat to get her attention.

She might have looked like a librarian sitting behind her desk, but the woman who walked over to the Arthur's door and stuck her head in his office, was definitely not a librarian. Although she was obviously in her fifties, she was wearing knee-high black boots, and a skirt that positively screamed "look at my legs"; the length of it a mere fraction of her waist size. I checked to see if Mel had noticed.

She had. "See something you like, Andy?" she asked, grinning at me. I knew that somehow I'd be punished for it. It didn't matter that I hadn't enjoyed it.

Mel had said it loud enough for the receptionist to hear, which was, no doubt, intentional. Fortunately, nothing showed that shouldn't have when the woman leaned into the doorway. Somehow she managed to turn around and tell us we could go in while still leaning over. As we walked past her into Arthur's office, she tipped her head down demurely and smiled,

I'd spoken with Arthur Eams on the phone, but this was the first time I'd met him. He didn't get up when we entered his office, but he did give us the phony smile of a long-time salesman as he gestured toward two chairs across from his desk.

He gave Mel a slow once-over as she sat down. "Who," he asked me, "is the good-looking girl?"

I introduced Mel as my wife rather than my assistant, thinking it would discourage any further inappropriate comments.

Arthur had draped the jacket of his brown polyester three-piece suit over the back of his chair. The buttons on his vest strained to hold back his soft, amorphous form, like a water balloon wearing a suit two sizes too small. His blue shirt was unbuttoned part-way, displaying a small tuft of wiry, red chest hair. Pink edged eyes peered out at us from a fleshy, round face crowned by a head of curly red hair.

His short stubby fingers tapped impatiently on his desk. "I hope you've got good news for me, 'cause I sure could use some."

"Actually, Arthur, I have a few questions, but first I need your signature on this." I handed him a piece of paper from my brief case.

He frowned.

I slid the paper across the desk toward him. "You don't mind if I call you Arthur, do you?"

He glanced at the paper. "What's this?"

I told him it was a standard attorney-client form. If I hadn't known better, I might have thought he was illiterate the way he looked at it, hardly what I'd expected from a guy who routinely handled landlord contracts. I told him to sign by the "X." He scribbled a messy signature on it without reading it. When I recommended that he read it, he waved his hand dismissively.

I replaced the form with a bill for my retainer. "That's my fee, Arthur. A check will be fine."

He wrote a check without blinking at the amount. Then as he handed me the check, his attention turned back to Mel. When she's annoyed she looks off into space. Arthur had noticed her looking over his head, mistaking Mel's annoyance for interest in the extensive display of auto parts calendars on the wall behind him. Grease smudges on some of the posters suggested that, at one time, they had actually hung on the walls of auto repair shops. All of them featured scantily-clad women in suggestive poses.

Apparently he only saw what he wanted to see in Mel's expression, because the last time I'd seen that one she was cleaning the cat's litter box.

"Nothing like good-looking women to dress up a wall," he said.

Arthur probably mistook the blush in Mel's cheeks for embarrassment. I knew it was anger, but angry as she was, Mel kept her cool. "I don't know what to say, Mr. Eams."

"I've got more at home," he said. "What I can't believe is that some people actually throw them away. I figure they're gonna be worth something someday."

Mel sat there with a blank look on her face as though she'd been given a general anesthetic. Her opinion of Arthur would've been low enough to start with; he didn't need to throw manure on it. The man was much too excited about the calendars, and much too interested in Mel.

Arthur rambled on about the calendars, oblivious to Mel's discomfort. "Someday one of those high-priced women's magazines is gonna run an article about calendars like these. It's gonna say they're nostalgic. Then the same women who've been making us take them down will be paying good money for them. I'll enjoy the irony in that."

Undeterred by Mel's stone-faced countenance, he said, "If

31

you see one you like, I'll give you a good price on it."

Having just been arrested for his wife's murder, a murder for which he had no convincing alibi, but for which there was some rather compelling circumstantial evidence against him, Arthur was seemingly oblivious to his rather dire predicament. I envied his ability to ignore the freight train about to squash him. And I appreciated his willingness to pay my fee. So I didn't much care that Arthur chose to live in a world clearly detached from reality. Unfortunately, he had riled Mel and she would redirect her anger toward me after we left his office.

In the meantime, I had to get him to focus. "Arthur this isn't a social visit."

He scowled. "I wrote you a check. What else can I do for you, Mr. Lee?"

"You can start by telling me how your car ended up at the murder scene."

"You didn't read the statement I gave the police?"

"I did." I wanted Mel to watch Arthur's expressions as he told his version of what had happened. "Humor me, Mr. Eams."

"It couldn't have been my car because I wasn't there."

"Someone saw it."

"They were mistaken."

"Arthur, what are the chances there's another dark blue Lincoln with a roof like that in a small town like Ithaca?"

Arthur leaned forward, putting his elbows on his desk. "Try to look at this from my point of view, Mr. Lee. I drove my car to the club that night, and I was there all night. So it couldn't have been my car?"

"Your car would be hard to mistake, even at night."

"I shouldn't have to tell you how to do your job, Mr. Lee."

"And just what does that mean?"

"Someone must've seen my car parked at the club. I suggest you find him."

"If he can be found, I will."

"Are we done, Mr. Lee?"

"According to the police report, your wife was seeing

someone else."

"So?"

"So why'd you go to her boyfriend's house?"

"I already told you. I was at the club the night Sheila was killed."

"Maybe you weren't there that night, but you were there."

"That's no secret. Hell, I'm the one who put it in the police report."

"They found your prints all over the boyfriend's house. How do I explain that to a jury?"

"I went there hoping to catch them in the act, but they weren't there. So I had a look around."

"Apparently you did a lot of looking."

"I wanted to see what the competition had to offer her, wouldn't you?"

"No Arthur, I wouldn't, and I hope you understand how problematic that's going to be for your case."

"Forget the fingerprints, Mr. Lee. Tell me why I'd kill my wife instead of her boyfriend."

"The DA could argue that you went there intending to kill the boyfriend, but that he wasn't there and your wife was, that you got into an argument with her and killed her."

"Hey I've got an idea, Mr. Lee. Find out whose car that was at her boyfriend's house. Then you'll have your murderer."

"One more question, Arthur."

"Shoot."

"How'd you get a copy of the boyfriend's house key?"

"I'm a landlord. I'm in the repo business. I copy keys all the time. I made a copy of my wife's."

I asked him how he knew where her boyfriend lived.

"I had her followed."

"That's not good, Arthur."

"Why?"

"The DA will tell the jury that copying the key and having your wife followed shows premeditation."

"It doesn't sound so good when you put it that way. But

that's why I hired you instead of using a public defender."

"Well, unless we get a break, you're looking at some serious time."

He pushed his chair back from the desk and put his feet up on it. "I left something out of the police report."

"What?"

"I've got an alibi."

"You mean someone from the Tender Loin? That won't do you any good unless you can prove that you were there at the time Sheila was killed."

"I can."

"How?"

"I was there all night with a girl named Ginger. She works there. Talk to her. But don't let the management know your sniffing around, or there'll be hell to pay for the poor girl. After you talk to her, come back and we'll have a meaningful conversation."

"She's a stripper?"

"Yeah. Is that a problem?"

"Then there's a chance she's either a prostitute, or a drug addict, or both."

Arthur scowled at me. "What's your point, Mr. Lee?"

"If she's the only thing between you and going to prison, then you should get yourself some KY." I had no sooner made the remark than I regretted it. It wasn't like me to be disrespectful to my clients, even if it was true.

Arthur stared at me, a well-rehearsed, angry landlord stare I suppose. "Are we done now?" he asked.

"Is there something you're not telling me, Arthur? If there is, you can bet it'll come out during the trial."

The fabric of his vest puckered, the buttons straining to contain his doughy bulk as he took in a deep breath. "I got mad and went over there when I found out Sheila was having an affair."

He paused, his throat working as though he was having difficulty swallowing. "Sorry, but I still can't talk about her like

34

she's gone."

He sounded sincere to me but I'm a poor judge of that. Mel would tell me later if Arthur's display of grief was genuine.

"In spite of what you might've heard," Arthur said, "I did love my wife. But over the years we drifted apart."

Mel stiffened ever so slightly then said, "Cheating on each other is not drifting apart."

That took Arthur by surprise. I happened to agree with Mel, but I didn't want her views on fidelity sidetracking the conversation. "Arthur, by using Ginger as your alibi you'd be admitting that you cheated on your wife. That could turn some jurors against you."

"And I worry what'll happen to Ginger if it does come out."

"For now she's the only thing between you and prison."

After a few seconds of finger tapping, Arthur said, "And we're wasting precious time, time you should be spending on my defense. I hope you'll have better news for me next time."

I told him I'd give him weekly updates then stood up to leave.

He stood up and reached across the desk, offering to shake my hand. "No reason we shouldn't be friends."

Mel usually keeps a poker face when we meet with clients, but she grimaced when Arthur offered to shake my hand. It felt as soft and damp and warm as fresh bread dough. As I shook it I told him I preferred to keep things on a professional level.

"I am sorry to hear that, Mr. Lee. But if that's the way you want it, then so be it."

Mel hurried to the door to avoid shaking Arthur's hand. Although the sky outside was still the uniform off-white color of impending rain, there was a chance the weather might improve, unlike the outlook for either of my cases.

CHAPTER V

Before Mel started the car she asked me if the Eams case was worth the money.

"Last time I checked, Hon, we still get bills in the mail."

As she pulled out of the parking lot onto Taughannock Boulevard heading south, she said, "That guy's going to prison."

"Case closed, simple as that?"

"He's guilty as hell, Andy, I can feel it."

"I could use something more specific?"

"He's the bogyman hiding in the closet."

"That doesn't help."

"He's as creepy as they come."

"Last time I checked, being creepy isn't a crime."

"Well, it should be."

As soon as I told her to ease up, I knew I'd made a mistake, because I felt the car speed up a little. She did that when she got mad, so I didn't need to hear it in her voice, even though it was there. "I hate it when you say that, Andy. It's like telling someone not to cry."

"Sorry, Hon, it's just that this guy Eams is a saint compared to some of the creeps I've dealt with over the years."

She changed the subject on me. "Did you see the way he was stuffed into that suit, like uncooked sausage? How do I get that image out of my head?"

"Don't you think that's a little extreme?"

36

"You'd think so too," she said, "if you didn't have the fashion sense of a junkyard dog."

"Could we get back to Arthur's case, Hon?"

"Just don't ask me to go back to his office."

When her speed and her anger both slackened a few blocks later, she asked me how I planned to handle his case."

"Well, I don't actually know whether or not he did it."

She smiled. "I am so glad to hear you admit that he could be guilty."

After we had crossed the bridge over the canal, Mel turned south on the four-lane, so she could drop me off at Morey's to get my car.

As she parked behind my car, she said, "Arthur insisted he was at that club when his wife was murdered."

"Yeah, what's your point?"

"How long was he there?"

"All night, assuming he was telling us the truth."

"That place is open all night?

"I doubt it."

"Then what was he doing there all that time?"

"I assume he was having sex with Ginger."

I noticed a shudder work its way from her head all the way down to her legs, punctuated with, "Oh, yuck."

"Girl's gotta make a living, Mel."

Her voice took on an edge. "Help me understand what you'd lose if you gave up this job."

If I was honest about it, I'd have to admit she was right, but I didn't want to go where that road led, so I changed the conversation back to the dancers at the club Arthur frequented. "The girls at the Tender Loin are strippers. No doubt some of them are also prostitutes. They pass through small towns like Ithaca, working at places like that because it's safer than walking the streets in a big city. If they get rousted by the authorities they move on to the next town down the Greyhound line."

"Those poor girls. I've driven past that place a hundred times, but I never gave a thought to what goes on in there."

"Mel, there are people out there who've been mistreated in ways you and I can't imagine."

She asked me if the police knew what went on there.

"Prostitution isn't popular with the voters, but it's easier and cheaper for the city to confine it to a few out of the way places than it is for them to eliminate it."

As I was getting out of the car she asked me what the place was like.

"What do you mean?"

"How do they arrange for the sex?"

"You'd have to ask Arthur that."

She looked at me with a faint trace of a smirk. "Lucky for you, you didn't know the answer."

I gave her a peck on the cheek and wondered if she would've asked the question if she'd been worried about my answer. A bright patch of sunlight on the pavement, created by a break in the clouds, slid past me as I walked to my car. Dry, copper-colored leaves scraped along the pavement, carried across the parking lot by a light breeze, the same breeze that ruffled the hair on my arms and brought the smell of cooking fat to me from the diner.

From Dorris' I drove across town to my office on Aurora Street. Located in the downstairs of a period, Georgian-style house, it was only two blocks from the courthouse. Floor-to-ceiling windows, both upstairs and down, were shaded by maple trees in the summer, but flooded with winter sunshine after the trees dropped their leaves.

Mel and I had lived in the upstairs apartment for a few years when I started my practice. Although we'd moved to the suburbs years ago, we still spent an occasional evening there for old times' sake, and it was a great place to go for some peace and quiet during a stressful day.

When it was built in the mid-eighteenth century it had four bedrooms upstairs. We sacrificed two of them for closets and a bathroom. The master bedroom, which was at the front of the house with windows overlooking the street, became our living room. The new kitchen was too small for serious cooking because part of it had been sacrificed for the bathroom, but it was convenient for preparing light meals. The furniture consisted mostly of pieces we'd brought from our new house as we upgraded the furnishings there, so it was an eclectic mix of traditional quality and modern convenience spanning more than a century.

I drove around to the parking area behind the house to use the back entrance so I wouldn't have to walk through the waiting room. A few minutes after I got settled at my desk my phone rang, a glowing status light indicating an outside call. I let my secretary take it. My phone rang again a moment later, the light for my secretary's line coming on, so I picked up. "Yes, Anne."

"Oh good, you're here, Andy. I've got a Mr. Reed on line one. Can you take it?"

I was tempted to tell her no because I already had enough clients to pay the bills. "Did he say what he wanted?"

"He said he had information about Dean. He said you'd want to hear it."

"Thanks Anne, I'll take it."

I punched the button for line one. "What've you got for me, Mr. Reed?"

"Not over the phone. Meet me at the D&P warehouse on Spencer Street tonight at seven."

I sometimes get calls from con artists trying to sell me useless information. "How much is this going to cost me?"

"I don't need money. I need protection."

"What is it you know that put you in danger?"

"I was with Dean when he kidnapped that girl."

I didn't tell him that I'd already decided to meet him. "I need more than that, Mr. Reed."

"He's got a hunting cabin on Halsey Road out past Enfield Center. I think that's where he took her."

Before hanging up he said, "Check it out, and be there at seven 'cause I've got plenty more to tell."

Spencer Street was not the best place to meet someone after dark, especially a stranger. But since it was my first and only real lead, I scribbled the place and time on a scrap of paper and stuffed it in my pocket.

Then Dean cast a dark shadow on my day. I needed to talk with the DA about his case. I buzzed Anne and asked her to come to my office. She'd always been such a dependable and efficient secretary that I tended to take her for granted, and isn't that the danger of being good at your job? I have also tended to forget how professional both her deportment and appearance are, and how that reflects positively on my practice.

When she got to my office I asked her to call Francis and arrange a meeting. "Doesn't matter where, but the sooner the better."

"Will do, Andy. And by the way, a Mrs. Jennings has been waiting to see you for over an hour."

Anne lowered her voice almost to a whisper, although the waiting room was down the hall and the door was probably closed. "She wouldn't say what she wants but she did say she's not leaving until you see her."

I had no illusions about Mrs. Jennings opinion of me. Even if she knew something that would help me, I doubted she'd share it with me after what Dean did to her and her daughter.

CHAPTER VI

I told Anne to send Mrs. Jennings in, adding, "Do me a favor and interrupt us in about five minutes, because I'm not sure I can get out of this gracefully on my own. Make up something if you have to."

"That bad, Andy?"

"Yeah. That bad."

As Anne's footsteps faded, I heard her say something to someone in the waiting room, then heard two sets of footsteps approaching and felt my blood pressure rising. At first glance Mrs. Jennings looked too young to be Sara's mother. But a more careful look revealed lines at the corners of her mouth where hairline cracks had formed in her makeup, like fracture lines in drying mud. Up close, she would've looked better without the makeup.

I heard somewhere that you can tell when an older woman was in her prime from her makeup style, and Mrs. Jennings' makeup looked like my mother's. She might not fool anybody with her face paint, but her silky, close-fitting, lilac-colored dress draped a slender body that would be the envy of women twenty years younger, the gently swishing fabric exaggerating the sway of her hips. Thin chains of tiny, clear crystals hung from her ears, flickering with rainbow colors in the sunlight coming through the window behind her.

I gave her a moment to get settled in my guest chair before asking her, "What can I do for you, Mrs. Jennings?"

Rather than meet mine, her eyes settled on something

41

slightly lower. I wondered if there was a stain on my shirt. When she spoke, her voice was barely audible. "I'm Sara's mother."

"Yes, ma'am, I know."

Her words came out fitfully, almost painfully. "Do you have any idea... how hard this has been... for me, Mr. Lee?"

I told her I couldn't imagine her pain, after which we sat there silently for a few very uncomfortable moments. Eventually she handed me a large manila envelope. "I brought you a picture of Sara. I want you to put it on your desk where you'll see her every day. That's not too much to ask, is it, Mr. Lee?"

"I am sorry, Mrs. Jennings, but that would be unprofessional."

I should have lied to her, agreeing to display it then putting it in a drawer after she left, because my comment doused her fire with gasoline. "How can you say that after what Dean did to my little girl?"

She had a point, but so did I. "Mrs. Jennings, if the judge isn't satisfied with my performance as Dean's defense counsel, he could declare a mistrial, setting Dean free. Neither of us wants that."

Her lips moved. I heard a dry guttural rasp. I asked her if she wanted some water, but she just looked down at her lap, eyeing her hands as she rubbed them together. When she caught me looking at them, she held them still. That's when I heard familiar footsteps in the hall and knew Anne was coming, bless her heart.

Anne's knock sounded as loud as a gunshot. Still, the relief from the tension was much appreciated. "Come in, Anne."

She opened the door and leaned in to say, "The DA is on the line. He said it's important."

Then she stepped back into the hall and held the door open, an invitation for Mrs. Jennings to follow her out. She did so without making any further eye contact with me. I heard the two women walk out to the reception area, then, moments later, I heard Anne coming back.

She knocked and stuck her head in the door. "You okay,

Andy?"

"Yeah, fine. Thanks, Anne."

She asked me what I thought of Mrs. Jennings.

"She must have been attractive once, but in ways that probably appealed to the wrong people. Why do you ask?"

"I was thinking something along those same lines. And, by the way, you're on with Francis, two o'clock this afternoon, his office."

Next, I called a guy I used for my more dangerous or arduous work, a diamond-in-the-rough named Rick Aiello. I asked him to meet me at six at his favorite restaurant, the Sicilian Carryout on north Meadow Street.

After that I took a minute to enjoy the view out my office window. The leaves on the majestic old maple trees lining the driveway between my office and the house next door have an amazing range and depth of color. Looking at them through the antique, rippled glass in my office windows, was like looking at an impressionist painting.

I got to the DA's office at two o'clock exactly. It's never bothered me when other people were late, but being late myself has always made me anxious. No doubt there's a self-help guide out there somewhere that addresses my problem, but if self-help books really worked, we'd stop buying them. So I suppose their very existence is proof they don't work?

The DA's secretary had always been curt with me. Maybe she was unhappy working for hFrancis. Maybe she'd picked up on his low opinion of defense attorneys. Maybe she just didn't like me. Regardless, all she said was, "He's busy," as though that was all the courtesy I deserved. I took a seat and pretended to read one of the out-of-date magazines on the display rack.

Francis Ewing had been the district attorney here for as long as I could remember. Physically a big man, but morally a small one, he aspired to a much loftier position, one more in line with his bloated self-importance.

When her line buzzed, I looked at his secretary. She looked back at me with the kind of disdain usually reserved for

43

homeless people. She pointed to Francis' office. I felt like a child being sent in to see the principal.

Francis was waiting for me behind a massive, old oak desk with nothing on it but a matched set of very expensive-looking silver desk accessories, and the obligatory photograph of his wife and kids that all politicians have on their desks. An eye-catching floor lamp with a Tiffany style, stained-glass globe that, knowing Francis, may have actually been the real thing, stood in the corner.

His law book collections lined the floor-to-ceiling bookshelves of his office, except for a few small groupings of them that were distributed around the office where they appeared to have been used recently as reference books. Thing was; those groupings hadn't moved in all the years I'd known Francis. So I suspected they'd been arranged for photo ops. Francis often invited reporters to his office for interviews, hoping to get newspaper coverage.

With a full head of wavy black hair and just enough gray showing on the sides to lend him some undeserved credibility, Francis was as well-groomed as any politician. His cheeks had the rouge tint of someone who'd just came back from a brisk walk on a cold day. Wearing a dark suit that looked much too expensive for a DA's pay scale, he exuded casual confidence, that hard-to-achieve look often an affectation of people born, as he was, to wealth and privilege.

He waved at me dismissively, as though I was no more than a pesky child. "If you're here to talk about a deal for Dean or Eams, you're wasting my time, Andrew."

I harbored no illusions that he'd be willing to cut a deal on the Dean case but asked him to consider one anyway. Sometimes my willingness to invite humiliation even surprises me.

I'd barely gotten Dean's name out before Francis said, "I'd be crazy to consider a deal on the Dean case? Hell, a first year law student could close that one."

Bargaining is not a lot of fun when you don't have anything to bargain with, so I went fishing. I asked him why he hadn't charged Dean with molesting Sara.

He leaned forward in his chair, resting the elbows of his designer suit on his blotter, looking over the tops of his bifocals at me. "What's the rush? He's not going anywhere, but you are, because you've overstayed your welcome, Andrew."

It hit me then why Francis hadn't charged Dean with raping Sara. He was going to keep that card up his sleeve. He would use it when it would get him maximum play with the voters, not to mention a good photo op.

I was trying to come up with an argument that might persuade Francis to cut a deal on Dean, when he cocked his head at a slight angle. "Are you hard of hearing, Andrew?"

"Tell me Francis, does your recalcitrance have anything to do with your re-election?"

He stood up and tossed his pen on his blotter. "Do you need help finding the door?"

That was my clue to leave. I really can take a hint, but I didn't want word getting back to Dean that I hadn't made a reasonable effort to get him a deal. Honestly, I was glad Francis wouldn't consider a deal.

After the demoralizing chat with Francis, I wanted to recharge my batteries, so I walked from the courthouse back to my office on Aurora Street to get my car. Then I drove north on Aurora toward the lake, passing through an area the locals call "the flats". Several square miles of wetland at the southern end of Cayuga Lake had been filled in sometime in the early nineteenth century, eventually becoming quaint, tree-lined, working-class neighborhoods.

I pulled into Stewart Park, driving past the pavilions and the children's play area. I can still remember running through the water fountains there on hot summer days. The concrete slabs for the fountains, still embedded in the grass, looked like short sidewalks to nowhere. And the city had replaced the grand old carousel I rode on as a child with a new, smaller one, which they seldom ran. But it was a peaceful, stress free place for me to enjoy some down time.

Along the shoreline, half a dozen squeaky bench swings hung on rusty chains in wood frames. I found an empty one and set it in motion. Leaning back with my eyes closed, soothed by the sounds and smells of the park, shedding my troubles as easily as a tree sheds its leaves in an autumn wind.

I heard waves lapping against the shore, gulls flying overhead squawking for handouts, excited noisy children, and the squealing chains of the swing. I smelled fresh cut grass and the stagnant water of the shallows along the shoreline.

Fed by countless streams flowing into it from the surrounding hills, Cayuga Lake sits in a forty-mile-long basin that was carved by a retreating glacier after the last ice age. At the time of the murder and kidnapping we hadn't had a hard frost yet, but the leaves had started to change color and a few had already fallen. In the next few weeks, Mother Nature would paint the surrounding hills in a luxuriant palette of fall colors. And cool dry air would blow in from Canada making the heat and humidity of summer just a fading memory.

When I got back to the office, I looked through the Eams case file to find out where Daren Miller, Mrs. Eams' boyfriend, worked. Then, after checking with Anne to be sure I wouldn't miss anything important, I called Mel and asked her to come get me. I waited for her at a picnic table we had set up under the maple trees behind the office.

CHAPTER VII

Mel was wearing a white blouse and a mid-calf, dark blue skirt when she arrived a few minutes later. She smiled at me as I settled into the passenger seat. "This is a nice surprise. What's the occasion?"

"I haven't seen your pretty face in a while."

"Good answer," she said. "But really, where are we headed?"

"Ithaca Power and Light."

"Paying our utility bill in person wasn't what I had in mind when I suggested we get out more."

"Daren Miller works there. I thought we'd pay him a visit."

"You are an incurable romantic, Andrew Lee."

"I know."

"Who's Daren Miller?"

"Boyfriend of the late Sheila Eams."

"Now you're talking my language."

A five mile drive out past the jail, put us in the parking lot of a big, rectangular, four-story office building. The uniformed guard sitting behind the counter in the lobby phoned Daren to tell him he had visitors. After signing the guest register we sat in the waiting area, a grouping of chairs and potted tropical plants that looked like an oasis in the otherwise big empty room.

Daren Miller showed up a few minutes later wearing a brown plaid shirt and dark slacks. Taller, leaner, and younger than Arthur, with striking, bright-blue eyes and a dense crop of wavy brown hair, he looked the antithesis of Arthur; small wonder Sheila found him attractive.

He greeted us with his arms folded across his chest. "I'm Daren Miller."

I proffered a hand for him to shake. "I'm Andrew Lee. This is, Mel, my assistant."

He ignored my hand. "I know who you are. I saw your picture in the paper."

Apparently more people read the local rag than I thought. "Then you know why I'm here."

Based on the curt manner in which he delivered his answer, I didn't expect much cooperation from him. "I already told the police everything I know,"

When I told him that one or two things in his written statement were unclear, he got testy. "The police were okay with it."

"You can answer my questions now or you can answer them when I put you on the stand. Your choice, Daren."

He told us to follow him then led us through a labyrinth of hallways, unlocking doors by inserting a plastic-coated card into little boxes mounted near the doorways. The last door opened into a long narrow room containing a dozen chairs crowded around a conference table; the kind of stuff you might see at an office furniture salvage store.

He sat down. Mel and I took seats across the table from him. He scratched his neck, leaving an angry looking patch of red skin. I hoped it meant we'd made him anxious, because people are more likely to deceive you when they're cool and calm and thinking clearly.

"I understand that you worked late the night Sheila was killed."

He shrugged his shoulders. "So?"

"How often do you work late?"

"Only when I have to," he said. "Why, what's your point?"

"Is there someone who can corroborate it?"

"Which part?"

"That you were told to work late."

"I wasn't."

"Then why'd you work late?"

"You're kind of clueless, aren't you, Mr. Lee?"

"Please answer the question, Mr. Miller."

"I had a deadline. I knew I wouldn't make it if I didn't stay late. And I still have a deadline, Mr. Lee, so let's wrap this up, shall we?"

I told him I'd be glad to save the rest of my questions for the courtroom.

He rolled his eyes and sat down. "Go ahead, ask away."

"According to your statement, your car wouldn't start when you quit work that night. So you called a tow truck. You took a cab home after they towed your car away, getting home sometime around two in the morning."

"Good for you, Mr. Lee; you can read for content."

"It sounds rather convenient."

"The guard at the front desk will have records of everything."

"Really?"

He tossed me a laminated card with a company logo on one side and his picture on the other, the same one he had used to unlock doors as we followed him in from the lobby. "The outside doors to this building are always locked and can only be opened with one of those cards. Every time I use it to open a door the security system records my card number, the ID of the door, and the time down to the second. There'll be an entry in the log for when I tried to leave, another one for when I came back in to call the tow truck, and another one for when I finally left for the night."

I asked him how I could get a copy of the logs. He told me to ask the guard then stood up again. "Now, are we done?"

"Sure."

He escorted us back to the lobby. We no sooner got back to the car than it started to rain, pounding on the roof, the sound as loud as if it had been pea gravel. Mel asked me if I believed his story about having a deadline, almost yelling to be heard above the rain.

"Would you mind calling personnel to get his boss's name, then calling his boss to ask if Daren really does have a deadline?"

"Did you think I'd enjoy doing that, or are you too cheap to pay your detective friend to do it?"

"Sorry, Mel. I thought you enjoyed being a dick."

"I'd rather you didn't call me a dick, even if you mean the detective type. As for the work, I only enjoy it if it enhances my heroine persona.

"Would it help if I paid you for your time?"

"I was just giving you a hard time. There was a time you would've known that."

"Sorry, Mel. This Dean thing has me on edge."

"Forget it. I'll make the calls. In the meantime, you didn't tell me what you thought of Daren's story."

"I think he might have used the security card system to create an alibi."

"You mind explaining that?"

"Give me a few minutes to finish working it out."

"Okay then," she said, "tell me where we're headed. You can explain on the way."

I pulled her hand away from the ignition. "I need to go back inside."

"Alright then, Andy, we'll wait and see if the rain lets up. Meantime, you can explain away."

"Assume he did something to his car when he came back from dinner so it wouldn't start. It's easy enough to do that."

"What good would that do?

"Now suppose he got his hands on someone else's security card."

I knew immediately that she'd figured it out, because her posture stiffened and her mind came out of the gate like a racehorse, running so fast her tongue got twisted trying to keep up. "If Daren got ahold of another card, he could have left, driven home, killed Sheila, and then sabotaged his car when he came back so he'd have to call for a tow, which would give him an alibi. You think that's what he did?"

"Maybe."

She asked me why I hadn't tried it out on him when I was questioning him.

"Because I didn't think of the card scheme until we were leaving."

"And how do we check that out?"

"First, I think I should check his story against a printout of the security log. And while I'm waiting for that, I'll ask the guard if anyone's reported a card lost or stolen."

"Hey, Andy," she said, "suppose he waited by an outside door for someone to come in or go out, and told them he'd forgotten his card?"

"Good thought, Mel. I suppose we can ask everyone whose card shows up on the log if they remember holding the door open for Daren that night."

I told Mel to wait there for me while I went back in to talk to the guard. "No point in both of us getting wet."

"You could've asked for the report on the way out, or did you want to get soaked."

"I was so absorbed figuring out the card scam that I forgot about the report."

I ran back inside, getting drenched on the way, the water dripping off my clothes and pooling on the lobby floor by my feet while I explained to the guard what I wanted. He had someone from HR come talk to me and give him their okay. Then he did something on his computer terminal. He told me it would take a few minutes to print. While we waited, I asked him if there had been any reports of lost or stolen cards.

He typed some commands on his terminal. "It would show on this display if one had been reported lost or stolen in the last month and there's nothing here."

While I waited for the report, several people came and went through the front door using their security cards. I asked the guard, "Couldn't someone unlock the door with their card and hold it open for someone else?"

He said doing so would violate company policy. I found it hard to believe that the fear of violating company policy would deter a killer.

Getting into Mel's car with wet clothes made her grumpy. "I hope it was worth getting my car seat wet."

I set the printout down on the seat between us. "Would you mind checking the entries on this, Mel?"

"Does my usual rate apply?"

"If by that you mean no money changes hands, then yes, it does."

"Gee, Andy, you sure you can spare it?"

"It's the least I can do, Hon."

"Truer words….and all that crap."

So much water was flowing down the windshield the world appeared to be melting. She asked me if I wanted her to stop at the house so I could change out of my wet clothes before she dropped me off at the office.

"Thanks, Mel, but there isn't enough time before I have to meet Rick."

And after my meeting with Rick, it would probably be time to go meet Mr. Reed. I hoped what he had to tell me would be worth the trip.

CHAPTER VIII

By the time I got to the Sicilian Carryout to meet Rick, the weather had cleared, but the weak autumn sun was about to set behind the western hills. I could feel the difference in temperature, the air having cooled considerably since Mel dropped me off at the office an hour earlier.

Rick considered the Sicilian Carryout a restaurant, but with just a few tables where people could sit to wait for their orders, it hardly qualified. It was located on the north side of Ithaca across the street from Purity Ice Cream, a popular ice cream parlor that had been in business since early in the prior century. Open year-round, the place was especially crowded on hot summer nights.

I sat near a window at the carryout so I could watch the crowd at Purity while I waited for Rick. He was easy to spot getting out of his car in new denims, shiny black shoes, and a snug fitting white tee-shirt.

Always bleached to a blinding white, and usually a size too small, his tee-shirts showed off his powerful-looking physique, the result of years of weight lifting. I wondered if Rick saw a young body builder looking back at him when he looked in the mirror, as though the glass bent time back in on itself just for him. Because both our looks and our eyesight normally deteriorate as we age, mirrors would be kinder to us if it wasn't for corrective eyewear.

Rick and I had shared an apartment before I went to law school. Rick doesn't have half the fashion sense that I have,

53

and I have none. The man is fastidious about his shoes and tee shirts, which are woefully out of style. He still puts on copious amounts of cologne, creating a scented gas cloud that precedes him wherever he goes and lingers after he leaves.

I saw him sitting in his car in the parking lot looking at himself in the rear view mirror of his car. He fussed with his thinning hair before he got out. As he walked in from his car he checked his reflection in the restaurant windows.

Because he had a big stupid grin when he sat down across from me, I suspected that he had mischief on his mind, and I was right.

He opened the conversation with, "I hear they opened a new strip club in Elmira. We could be there in thirty minutes."

As I fought back a sneeze brought on by his cologne, I told him, "Forget Elmira, we need to talk about the Arthur Eams case."

It'd be just like old times"

"I think you have me confused with someone else, Rick."

He held his hand up, catching the eye of a young woman working behind the counter. Although the Sicilian Carryout didn't actually have wait staff, she came over to our table to take our orders. Rick eats there so often, everyone who works there knows him. He ordered a sausage sandwich. She asked me if I wanted anything, I shook my head.

After she left, Rick asked, "You're still buying, right Andy, even if you don't eat anything?"

"Sure."

"We can talk about Eams' problem on the way."

It was easier to just ignore the suggestion. "They're going to give Arthur a very long stretch inside unless I can pull a rabbit out of my hat. That's where you come in."

Rick grinned then nodded in the direction of the woman who'd waited on us and made an inappropriate gesture with his hands regarding her ample bust then said. "Eams is gonna get what he deserves when some big ugly convict makes him his girlfriend."

"No doubt he has a debt to pay society, but I'm not so sure this murder belongs on his scorecard."

Rick's grin faded. "Maybe you're right, but you gotta ask yourself how those lofty moral values of yours have served you over the years."

"Meaning what?" I asked.

"Meaning, that the guy's no good and oughta be locked up."

Not in the mood for an argument over principles, I told him, "Arthur claims he has an alibi; a dancer named Ginger who works at the Tender Loin."

"That's not much of an alibi."

"He claims he was with her all night."

As the same waitress handed Rick his sandwich, he said, "Either this guy Eams has some serious money or a really big,..."

I knew what he was going to say next, so to save both myself and her some embarrassment I interrupted him. After she left Rick took the greasy sausage out of his sandwich and made a crude gesture with it. The open roll was drenched with a concoction of Italian dressing and tomato sauce.

I whispered so the people working behind the counter wouldn't hear me. "How can you eat that?"

"Watch me," he said, grinning like a fool to display a mouthful of sandwich.

Rather than watch him savage his sandwich, I went back to watching people come and go at the ice cream parlor across the road. A few of them sat outside at picnic tables even though it had to be uncomfortably cool now that the sun had set. I guessed that the parents chose to sit outside in the cold so their kids dripped melting ice cream on the picnic tables instead of their car's upholstery.

One of the drawbacks to living in a valley is that the sun always rises and sets behind a hill. So, early mornings and late evenings are cooler here. And instead of seeing sunrises or sunsets, the setting sun colors the sky and tints the surrounding hills with shades of red and pink.

While Rick brutalized his sandwich, I told him that Arthur was desperate and that, "He's got money. He'll pay generously for your help."

He put the last morsel of his sandwich down on his plate "What does he need me for if he's got an alibi?"

"You know that's a mixed bag at best. If they're lovers, which is a stretch, she'd have reason to lie for him, making her a poor witness. If they're not lovers then he's paying for the sex. That makes her a prostitute. Her reward for her honesty will be getting run out of town. And besides that, she'll be worried about the guy who owns the place, because he won't want her telling the world he's running a sex-for-hire business."

I happened to noticed that none of the greasy red sauce from his sandwich had ended up on his white tee shirt. "Why would you wear white knowing you'd be eating something with red sauce on it?"

For some reason I couldn't ascertain, he grinned then asked, "So you want me to talk to Ginger?"

"If Arthur was at the Tender Loin, I want to know when he got there, when he left, and if she was with him the whole time. Of course, none of that's any good unless she's telling the truth, so try to get a read on that."

"How am I supposed to do that?"

"I don't know, Rick. Get creative?"

"Yeah, sure, easy for you to say." Rick stood up to leave. "Thanks for dinner, Andy."

"Wait, Rick, there's one more thing. "Arthur's wife, Sheila, was murdered at her boyfriend's house."

"That's juicy."

"And the DA has a witness who saw Arthur's car parked across the street at the time she was murdered."

"They're sure it was his car they saw?"

"It's a dark-blue Lincoln with a custom top."

"Custom how?"

"As in, it has vinyl on the back half of the roof. I want you to find out if it's the only one like it in the area."

"Who'd be dumb enough to drive an easily recognizable car to a murder?"

"Hopefully not my client?"

Rick slid out of the booth. "Looks bad for this Eams fellow, Andy."

I paid for his dinner on the way out. By then it was almost six-thirty, time to go meet Reed. On the way to my car I saw remnants of the setting sun tinting the clouds above West Hill a dozen shades of pinks and reds. It looked like a water color painting.

From the Sicilian Carryout I drove to a small run-down industrial area southeast of Ithaca dominated by a five-hundred-foot-long factory building located high up on South Hill where it could be seen from anywhere in Ithaca. Already a blight on the landscape, it had been empty and decaying for years. I wondered what it would look like in another ten years.

The Ithaca area enjoyed a period of rapid industrial growth during the blue-collar boom of the fifties. Then it died a slow, agonizing, fiscal death as local jobs relocated to countries offering cheaper labor. Many of the buildings in the area had decayed for the same reason; including D&P Trucking's warehouse. I pulled into a parking lot that abutted three sides of the four-story warehouse. Full height windows reflected the pinks and reds in the clouds over West Hill.

I parked in front of an open overhead door. Either Reed was late or he had walked to our meeting, because the parking lot was empty. Because it was a dangerous neighborhood and almost dark, I decided to give him ten minutes, then leave.

The dim light of the setting sun overshot the bottom of the valley. In shadow, the warehouse doorway looked too much like a big black maw. A gust of wind blew an assortment of paper litter into the chain link fence at the other end of the parking lot. Some pieces hung there for a moment, plastered against the fence by the wind, before floating down to mix with the other trash snagged on the fence.

A derelict came into view down the street walking

unsteadily, his faltering gait no doubt the result of consuming whatever was inside the brown paper bag he was carrying. As I watched him approaching, a jacked-up, blue, four-wheel-drive pickup truck turned onto the street, coming toward me for half a block, before making a 'K' turn. It went back to the corner then turned right, disappearing down the side street.

I'd been thinking about the Eams case and security cards until I spotted the truck. It brought my attention back to the warehouse. I checked the dashboard clock. I'd already been waiting for Reed for nearly ten minutes. I wasn't surprised; informants aren't the most reliable people in the world. I thought about Reed mentioning Dean; about how dangerous Dean could be, and that no one knew where I was. It wasn't the smartest way to end what had already been a bad day. My instincts told me to leave. I should have trusted them.

CHAPTER IX

With no other leads in the case, I decided to give Reed the benefit of the doubt and go see if he was waiting for me inside the warehouse. I got out of the car reluctantly, taking my time walking to the overhead door, hoping Reed would show up before I set foot in the cavernous darkness. He didn't.

Standing ten feet inside the door I paused to let my eyes adjust to the dim interior, the weak evening light barely penetrating the grime coated windows. Rows of truck-size storage crates piled several stories high receded into the obscure recesses of the building.

When I yelled Reed's name, I heard a faint echo of myself yelling his name. Waiting any longer for Reed seemed foolhardy; it would be dark in a few minutes and he was one of Dean's associates, so there was no telling what crimes he had on his resume.

I had decided to leave because something didn't feel right. It was one of those irrational feelings that give you a chill on a hot day, or make you think a bug's crawling up your neck. Then I heard faint footfalls. I listened closely for a moment to get a sense of where the sound was coming from before walking deeper into the building.

About forty feet in I stopped just before a cross aisle to listen for the footsteps. Stepping cautiously around the corner into the cross aisle. I saw motion and that's the last thing I remember until I woke up on the floor with a throbbing headache. Too lightheaded to stand, I sat there until the dizziness passed and I felt steady enough to walk. I checked my wallet. Nothing was missing, but I'd been a fool and was paying for it with a headache.

I didn't waste any time getting back to my car. Driving out of the lot, I spotted the same pickup truck I'd seen doing a 'K' turn earlier. It was parked half-a-block away under a streetlight. I slowed to get the license plate number, but in the shadow of the truck, and conveniently dirty, it was unreadable, so I got out of there.

Before giving up on the day I decided to try one more thing. The police report mentioned a couple who had seen a van parked outside their house the night the Jennings girl was kidnapped. Thinking that a quiet ride might ease my headache and settle my nerves, I drove to the scene to look around.

Most of Ithaca's old cobblestone streets had long since been covered over with asphalt. The section of State Street running up East Hill was one of the few stretches of roadway that hadn't been resurfaced yet, rattling my car unmercifully as I drove up the steep grade toward Cornell University.

Half a mile up the hill the street veers to the right and levels out, becoming East State Street. Majestic old trees line the street, their branches arching high above the roadway, suggesting a fairytale-like covered forest path. If it weren't for a steady stream of cars, one might imagine horse-drawn carriages rumbling along to the sound of clacking hooves.

About a mile further out, I turned left onto Woodcrest Avenue which took me farther up the hill. The next left turn put me on Eastwood Avenue where Sara had been kidnapped. Many of the houses in the area were originally owned by Cornell professors. But as the status and wages of their profession rose, and the neighborhood's grandeur faded, the Cornell crowd moved to more fashionable locations. They were backfilled by blue collar workers.

I pulled over to the curb when I found Sara's friend's house, a small, well-kept, ranch-style house with a carefully-manicured little patch of lawn. I parked and left my car near there, retracing her steps toward the other end of the block. I would have appreciated a jacket against the cool night air.

Above me, puffy gray clouds racing across the black sky were backlit by a nearly full moon. I imagined a carefree young girl absently kicking the blanket of leaves on the sidewalk as she walked home. I wondered if she'd felt uneasy walking in and out of the darkness between the streetlights.

Instead of answers, my side trip paid off with a question—why didn't Dean park his van in the shadow cast by one of the big shade trees? Maybe Mike was right, maybe he was just another dumb criminal.

Ravenous by the time I got home, I was rummaging around in the refrigerator when Mel yelled to me from the other room. "You couldn't come say hello first?"

A plate of leftover meatloaf caught my eye. She came in while I was slicing up a large cholesterol-be-damned portion of it to make into a sandwich.

"So tell me," she said, as she sat down at the kitchen table.

"Tell you what?"

"What's new on the Eams front?"

I asked her to tell me about her day while I ate.

"If anything of interest had happened to me today I'd be glad to, but it didn't. So you're up."

I told her about not meeting Reed and that I had a headache, without explaining the connection between the two. She got me two Excedrin tablets. I sat down to eat my sandwich of meatloaf, French bread, and ketchup. Mel got a bottle of wine out of the fridge and popped the cork—great sound that.

She put two glasses of Bully Hill Chardonnay on the table then asked, "Have you decided how you're going to explain to a jury why the police found Arthur's fingerprints all over the boyfriend's house?"

I shook my head.

"And where did they find his prints?"

"On door knobs all through the house and on the dresser

61

drawer handles in the bedroom."

"God, he's creepy," she said, with an impressive full-body shudder.

"And it gets worse, Mel. He was there for a while, Mel. May have even been waiting for them to come back."

"I didn't think my opinion of him could get much worse, Andy, and yet it did."

"I agree, he's uncouth. But we can't let that cloud our judgment when it comes to his innocence."

"But it does, and you would do well to keep that in mind during jury selection."

"And do what exactly?"

"To minimize the risk of jurors being put off by Eams, pick as many slovenly candidates as possible."

"I knew I kept you around for a reason, Mel."

"You had to be reminded of that?"

I'd stepped into a minefield. I let the subject drop and worked on my sandwich.

By then she'd finished her wine and gone for a refill. "So what else is new, Andy?"

"According to the autopsy there weren't any signs of a struggle, meaning they didn't find any defensive cuts on Sheila's arms."

"Meaning that she didn't try to fight him off."

"Right, but it seems as though she'd at least try to defend herself, doesn't it, Mel?"

"Maybe she didn't get the chance."

"It's hard for me to imagine Arthur killing someone with a knife and not making a mess of it."

"So it's okay for you to make superficial judgments about Arthur, but you poo-poo it when I do."

"If it was up to you, Mel, you'd send him to prison for wearing a leisure suit."

"And you wouldn't? Are you kidding?"

Once again, I dropped the subject to focus on my sandwich.

Mel suggested that Arthur might have hired someone to kill his wife. "With his connections, he might know someone in the trade."

"Why would he allow someone to kill his wife at her boyfriend's house if his fingerprints are all over the place?"

"Maybe he neglected to tell the guy he hired not to do it at the boyfriend's place."

"What about the boyfriend's key? The police found it on Arthur's key ring. He didn't bother to take off. How much sense does that make, even if you allow for the fact that he's not the brightest star in the night sky?"

"You're scaring me, Andy. Next you're going to tell me he's innocent."

The sandwich had hit the spot; the wine, not so much. In the meantime, I appeared to have lost Mel, who was sipping her wine silently, seemingly deep in thought.

After a while she said, "Did anyone see him at that nightclub."

"I asked Rick to check on that."

"What about a credit card receipt?"

"You're kidding, right?"

That earned me a disapproving frown from Mel.

"Sorry, Hon. I assumed you knew."

"Knew what?"

"That the men who frequent places like the Tender Loin want it kept a secret. So places like that don't normally take credit cards, or checks, or reservations."

I got up to put my plate in the sink. Mel came and took it from me. "Go sit on the couch. You've had a long day."

I stepped behind her, pulling her to me, putting my arms around her. She pushed back against me, tipping her head back, rubbing her cheek against the side of my face. Later, curled up on the couch with Mel in a pile of pillows, my senses still fuzzy from the intimacy, I was only vaguely aware of my surroundings. Mel's face was a rosy red and her eyes had that dreamy, 'I can't quite focus' look.

She let out a sound that was something between a sigh and a moan. "We should do that more often."

Feeling lightheaded and unsure of my muscles, I followed Mel to the bedroom. Sleep came easily that night.

Frightened awake by a loud noise, I heard myself saying, "What the hell?" Then I heard the phone.

Mel poked me until I rolled over and answered it. "Who is this?"

"It's me, Rick."

I squinted at the clock across the room. "It's five in the morning."

He said, "I'm at Ginger's place," as though that excused the ungodly hour. "I think you're gonna like her, Andy."

Knowing I'd never get back to sleep I sat on the floor next to the bed. "Why the need to tell me this now?"

"She'll talk to us, but she wants money, not a lot of money, just a hundred dollars. Oh, and a bus ticket to Rochester."

"If I wanted money from you, I wouldn't call you at five in the morning to ask for it."

"I gotta go," he said. "She's coming out of the bathroom."

"She talks to us first," I told him, just before the dial tone cut me off.

Sleep was out of the question, so I decided to go to the office early before my nine o'clock meeting with Dean. But when I bent over to give Mel a kiss good-bye, she twisted around in the covers bunching her nightgown up around her thighs. I decided the office could wait.

Curled up under the sheets with Mel, listening to the wind gusting outdoors, and watching sun shadows playing on the walls, I was almost asleep when I heard the squeal of tires somewhere in the distance. It brought back my angst over the Dean case, a bad feeling of nausea and urgency that hit me like a mild case of food poisoning. With no hope of chance of regaining the serenity I'd lost when Rick called, I grabbed some clothes and made my way to the bathroom so I wouldn't wake Mel. Thinking about meeting Dean again did nothing for my queasiness, and the anxiety grew as I shaved and dressed.

CHAPTER X

The early Tuesday morning sun burned off the remnants of a thin wispy fog as I drove up East Hill to see Dean. I sat at the table in one of the interrogation rooms for what seemed an eternity before I heard chains rattling in the hallway. The guard stood inside the door. That was fine with me.

The chain between Dean's handcuffs and his leg irons forced him to bend forward, causing his arm muscles to knot and ripple as he walked. I told him Francis wouldn't agree to a deal. He glared at me with the intensity of a guard dog who'd caught me trespassing. "I know you talked to Jennings. No telling what'll happen to your wife if I find out you talked to her again."

Once again, I felt like I'd been punched in the gut. Dean had a way of doing that. I'd known that nothing good would come of Jennings' visit, but hadn't expected the trouble to come from Dean. I started to warn him off, but only got as far as saying, "Don't ever..." before I realized that nothing I said would have the desired effect.

He grinned at me then hobbled then hobbled out of the room. I went to see Mike. Although his office had a door, the glass wall around it afforded him little privacy. He waved me in when he saw me coming. "What's up, Andy?"

He must have had a late night or an early morning because his chin had the dark shade of an extra day's stubble. I told him I'd seen Dean again.

"Did that make your day, or what?"

66

"I've got a problem, Mike."

"You're not gonna give me a hard time because your boy's in chains, are you, Andy?"

I shook my head, but he had something he wanted to tell me, regardless. "Dean roughed up one of the guards last night, so I added an assault charge to his list of accomplishments."

"Whoa, Mike, I'm not here to complain about the chains. As a matter of fact, I'm glad he's out of action."

Pointing to a guest chair whose padding had given up the fight, Mike asked me what had gotten me upset.

I closed the door behind me, and sat down. "Dean threatened Mel. Normally I wouldn't worry too much about it, but he's obviously got somebody on the outside."

"What makes you think that?"

"Mrs. Jennings came to my office yesterday and Dean already knows about it."

"Then I'll have a patrol car keep an eye on your place. I'll have them go by Jennings' place too."

Having a patrol car drive by was less than reassuring. Of course, I didn't tell Mike that. I knew there wasn't much else he could do. Still, I'd worry about Mel being alone at our house.

"I wish I could do more, Andy. Hey, if it makes you feel any better, he rattles me too."

"Any idea why Dean wouldn't want me talking to Mrs. Jennings?"

"Guys like Dean keep coming back to stay with us, and frankly I doubt it's the food. But even if you put all of their bright ideas together, you'd still get more light from a safety match."

On that note, I left Mike's office. Outside, it was shaping up to be a beautiful early fall day in Upstate New York, with cottony white clouds suspended against a dark blue sky that matched the color of the lake, and a green blanket of trees, sprinkled with early fall colors, that filled the space between lake and sky. My angst had eased somewhat by the time I got to my office downtown.

I found three messages on my desk from Anne noting the

times Rick had called. When he called again a few minutes later he sounded harried. "Ginger's gonna help us out. But I've only got a minute, so I gotta make it quick."

I asked him where he was.

"We're someplace safe."

"Rick, please tell me you're not staying with her."

"I'm staying with her."

"What's your wife going to think when she finds out?"

"That's why I called. I need you call her and explain."

Rick had put me in some awkward situations over the years, but this crossed the line. "You want me to call your wife and tell her you're staying with a stripper?"

"No, I want you to make up something then call her. And think about what you're going to do with Ginger. She says she won't talk unless you can protect her, and I'll have to go home eventually."

"I'm not gonna lie to your wife, Rick. And as for Ginger, bring her to the apartment tonight at seven and we'll sort it out."

"You dog, I know what you're up to."

"No you don't. The apartment's a safe place to talk, nothing more. You make it clear to her that she's not getting any money or tickets unless she tells us the whole truth. You think she's capable of that?"

"I gotta go," was followed immediately by the dial tone.

As I wrote out a list of things I knew and didn't know about the Eams and Dean cases, I couldn't help thinking I'd missed something, that if I could just come at the questions from the right perspective, I'd see through the confusion. I also know you can't force something like that, so when I was still stuck an hour later, I put the exercise aside.

The rest of the day was uneventful; I actually made some progress with some of my more mundane casework. By five o'clock I was hungry, so I called Mel and asked her if she wanted Chinese, knowing full well she'd say yes. I picked her up at the house then headed downtown to the Dragon's Nest restaurant.

Although Ithaca's business district had changed

considerably since I was a kid, it still bustled at night. Most of the old businesses that were forced out by the chain stores on the four-lane had been replaced by specialty shops catering to tourists. The eclectic mix of high-end tourist shops and cooperative art galleries drew college alumni back to Ithaca.

Above Cayuga Lake and Ithaca, Cornell University sprawls across most of East Hill. Ithaca College sits high atop South Hill. A number of bars and restaurants catering to students are clustered within a bustling two-square-block area near where the bases of the two hills meet.

Occasionally Mel and I mixed with the younger crowd to try the food at one of the student hangouts. But our destination that night was our favorite Chinese restaurant several blocks away, a place so popular with both the locals and the students that it's difficult to find a parking place anywhere near it. I found a spot several blocks away. When we walked past a newspaper vending machine, I bought a copy. I wanted to know what the local paper was saying about my cases.

The Dragon's Nest restaurant is only about thirty feet wide but extends deep into the interior of the city block. Owned and operated by the grandchildren of the Chinese couple who opened the place in the nineteen forties, it had the atmosphere of a small, blue-collar American diner in spite of the numerous phony-looking Chinese decorations hanging on the walls.

The hostess asked us in broken English if we wanted tea.

We'd hardly had time to get settled before a waitress set a pot of tea and two demitasse cups made of think porcelain on the table between us.

Mel reached across the table to pat my hand. "Why don't we come here more often?"

CHAPTER XI

After Mel asked the waitress to bring us our usual, she asked me what I found so interesting in the newspaper.

I'd been so focused on reading the lead story that her comment startled me. "Sorry, hon."

"What planet are you on?" she asked.

I held the front page up so she could see the banner headline announcing another murder in Ithaca.

"Forget that, Andy. Let's just enjoy our dinners."

"That'll be tricky."

She waved her hand dismissively. "Why? You aren't mixed up in it."

"Actually, Mel, I am."

"How's that possible?"

I sipped some tea to quash the hunger pangs caused by the aromas wafting out of the kitchen. I told Mel that someone had found a dead body in a warehouse on Spencer Road.

"How's that your problem, Andy?"

"The dead guy's name is Reed. He asked me to meet him there yesterday."

"Please don't tell me you went there."

"I went there."

"Really, Andy?"

"He offered to give me information about Sara's abduction."

"So you met with the dead guy?"

70

"I didn't see him there so I left. Apparently he was there but not breathing."

"Well I hope you learned your lesson."

"Mel, I get calls all the time from people with information to sell. Most of them are nuttier than a bowl of trail mix. I wouldn't have bothered with Reed, but he claimed he was with Dean when Dean kidnapped Sara. He told me that Dean took her to a hunting cabin out near Enfield. Before he hung up he said he had more information but wouldn't share it with me over the phone."

Mel crossed her arms and leaned back in the booth. After a while she said, "I was thinking about Dean today, about his motive. It doesn't make sense."

"How's that?"

"Why would he risk prison time for kidnapping a teenage girl just so he can have sex with her mother?"

"Good question, Mel."

"The guy spent sixteen years in prison, Andy. Given sixteen years, an idiot could devise a better plan than that."

"How does that help me?"

Her bottom lip protruded a little after that. She sat there silently for a while, looking through the menu again, even though we'd already ordered. She'd made an astute observation and I should've given her more credit for it.

"So, Andy, this guy, Reed."

"What about him?"

"He told you Dean took Sara to a hunting cabin in Enfield."

"I don't suppose you'd want to go with me to check it out."

That got a smile from her. "And just this morning," she said, "I was thinking that you never take me anyplace fun anymore."

Then I told her about Dean's threat. She crossed her arms over her chest and glowered at me. I told her that Mike was having a patrol car keep an eye on our place.

"We both know that won't do much good, don't we, Andy?"

71

Then she lapsed into one of our old arguments. "You want to run some of that small town crap by me again, stuff like friendly and safe?"

I thought it wise not to answer. Meanwhile, she had redirected her frustration toward her purse, rummaging through it with grim determination, checking each compartment several times. After several minutes she let out a sigh then set it aside and changed the subject. "I'll bet you fifty dollars that Eams spends more time in jail than Dean. I'm having a hard time with that because Sara was just a kid. I don't have nearly as much sympathy for Sheila because she was dumb enough to marry Arthur."

The sudden topic change had given me a mental whiplash. Fortunately, the waitress arrived then, setting covered platters of fried rice and barbecued pork on our table. We ate in silence for a while. Mel finished first, then slouched down in the booth to sip her tea.

Her facial features had relaxed somewhat. I'm steady and predictable, and probably boring. Mel is mercurial, but she's also fun and exciting. I winked at her because I didn't know how else to hold on to the moment.

She looked at me askance. "I saw that."

I wondered if she gotten the message that I loved her. But moments later her expression changed, her lips closing so tight the color drained from them. She asked me why Dean had threatened her.

"Because I talked to Mrs. Jennings."

"So what?"

I held the empty teapot up to show the waitress before answering Mel. "I have no idea what's going on in his head."

"Are you going to talk to her again?"

"Dean wouldn't have made the threat unless Mrs. Jennings knows something that would be a problem for him."

Mel watched me work on the last of my fried rice. I do love the fried rice at The Dragon's Nest. After a while she said, "This must be hard on Jennings and her daughter."

"I can't imagine what they went through that night. And they've had to relive it again it every time someone has questioned them about it. It makes me wonder who's really being served by our system."

"Why, Andy," Mel said, smiling. "I think I detect a crack in that blind idealism of yours."

I told her not to read too much into it.

She broke the silence again a few moments later. "You know, if I were Dean I would've killed Sara and her mother."

"It's not like you to be so brutal, Mel."

"My point is: why would he leave witnesses, unless he wants to go back to prison? He doesn't want to go back to prison, does he?"

The waitress put two fortune cookies on the table between us. Mel, eagerly broke open one of the cookies and pulled out the fortune, but frowned when she read it. She handed it to me. "Why would she give me your fortune cookie?"

I read it out loud. "There's more insight in foresight than hindsight."

She pulled the fortune out of the other cookie. "Hey, no fair," she said, handing it to me, "this one is yours too."

It read, "Seek knowledge, for without it, there is no direction. Take action, for without it, there is no result."

I caught up with our waitress near the kitchen and asked her to bring Mel another fortune cookie. The waitress rolled her eyes playfully but obliged; we've always tipped generously.

After reading her new fortune, Mel said, "Well it's about time," then handed it to me.

Small wonder she liked it. I handed it back.

"No silly," she said, "you have to read it out loud."

"You are deserving of the highest praise and the deepest affection."

With a big, broad smile on her face, she said, "It goes without saying."

Instead of asking her the obvious - why she made me say it, I told her I thought mine were pretty good too.

"Oh, Andy, you can't be serious."

"Thing is, I feel as though I fell in a river and have been helplessly swept along by the current. So tomorrow I'm going to do the research I should've done before now. That covers the hindsight and the knowledge. Then, who knows, maybe some action will follow."

She winked at me. "I could use a little action."

I smiled, told her, "I like the way you think."

Sitting there, sipping tea with Mel gave me a much appreciated break from the gloom of the two cases looming over me. Unfortunately I had to tell her that Rick and Ginger were coming to the apartment. It would ruin the moment. I asked Mel if she remembered Eams telling us he was with a dancer at the Tender Loin when his wife was murdered.

She nodded but frowned. No doubt afraid I was going to take the conversation somewhere she wouldn't like. I knew better than to waste time trying to frame the news in a way she'd find acceptable. "Rick's bringing her to the apartment tonight."

I had expected to get a much sterner scolding than, "You should have checked with me before inviting her to our place?"

"I must say, Mel, you're taking it better than I expected."

"I'm being civil, Andy, because we're out in public. But we will replay this later."

"I have a favor to ask, Mel."

"You have the audacity to ask me for a favor now?"

"I want your impression of her."

"You want me there?"

It was a bit much to ask, but ask I did. Then she asked me if we had anything to drink at the apartment.

"Sorry Mel, but I want you stone, cold sober. I need to know if Ginger is telling the truth."

"I don't get it, Andy. You always know when I'm lying. Why can't you see it in other women?"

"Because you only lie to me when you're kidding around."

"How do you know?"

I realized that I didn't, which was unsettling. I checked my watch. "We should go. I told Rick to have her there by seven."

From where we parked, it was only five blocks to my office, but to ease congestion, the city had repurposed its two busiest thoroughfares as one-way streets, which meant we had to make a loop around the business district to get there. The circuitous route also meant that we had more time to enjoy the pleasant evening air blowing through the open car windows when we weren't stuck in traffic.

The cool, dry air also meant that the moon and stars were much clearer, so we took a minute to admire the night sky from the picnic table behind my office. When we got upstairs I called Mike at home to tell him about Reed.

He sounded irritated. "I guess you're not watching the Syracuse game."

"I wouldn't call you at home if it wasn't important."

"Okay, Andy, what's up?"

"I was at the D&P warehouse on Spencer Street last night."

"What on earth were you doing there?"

"Reed called me, asked me to meet him there. I thought he was a no-show so I left. But who knows, maybe he was there but couldn't come to the door."

"What'd he want from you?"

"He said he had information about Dean that I'd want to hear. He also mentioned that he needed protection."

"I guess he was right about that."

"So who is, or rather, was he?"

I heard the roar of fans cheering in the background. When it died down, Mike said, "He was a small-time repeat offender and general lowlife with a convictions sheet longer than my driveway. You have no idea what his information was?"

"Not a clue."

"So what you're saying, Andy, is that you went to a dangerous place after dark to meet a questionable character who might have had something of value to tell you. Does that sound about right?"

"It sounds foolish when you put it that way."

"Well, come in and give me a written statement in the morning. I'm missing a good game here."

After the call with Mike, I joined Mel in the kitchen. She was leaning over a map of the county she'd spread out on the kitchen table. "Where was it your dead friend said Dean took Sara?"

"My dead friend? Nice, Mel."

"Well?"

"He thought Dean took her to a hunting cabin somewhere near Enfield Center. I think he said Halls Road or maybe it was Hallstead Road."

"You didn't write it down?"

"Had I known someone was going to kill him I would have."

"Well I don't see Halls or Hallstead, but there is a Halsey Road."

"Well, maybe that's it."

Mel leaned over the map, her fingers floating over the countryside south of Ithaca, near Enfield Center. She tapped a spot on the map with her index finger. "That's somewhere out here."

"So?"

"So the bookstore over on Cayuga Street sells county maps that show a lot more detail, even some houses. I'm gonna call and see if they're still open."

"Hon, we have to wait here for Rick and Ginger."

"No, Andy, you have to wait for them. I won't be gone long."

I didn't want her walking across town by yourself after dark, but I knew trying to talk her out of it would be a waste of time. She looked up the number and called the book store. When she got off the phone, she grabbed her purse and coat and bounded down the back stairs, yelling up to me, "They're closing soon. Be back in fifteen."

I ran after her, catching her half a block away, pulling her close to me. "Remember Dean's threat."

76

"And do what?"

"Be aware of your surroundings and the people in them."

She gave me a peck on the cheek and was gone. I watched her until she turned the corner at the end of the block. I don't know how I got wired this way, but I'm one of those people who always finds something to worry about, and after what had happened to Reed I had good reason to worry.

CHAPTER XII

While I waited for Mel to return I tried to figure out how I could take the initiative on either the Dean case or the Eams case. But I was too worried about Mel to concentrate, so I wrote a note for Rick then went to look for Mel.

In the clear moonless night, the Milky Way looked like a handful of rock salt thrown across a piece of black felt. As I walked west from my office to follow Mel's route, a leaf with no more control over its destiny than I seemed to have, drifted down and collided with my coat, clinging to it precariously for a moment before sliding off.

When I turned the corner at the intersection of Aurora and State Streets, I spotted Mel about a block away, too far away for her to hear me yell over the noise of the traffic. Standing still with her head down, she was rummaging through her purse for something and didn't see me.

I also spotted someone coming around the corner from Cayuga Street half a block behind her. Whoever he was, he stopped short when he rounded the corner and saw her standing there. If he was following her he was an amateur. A pro would have casually walked past her to avoid suspicion.

Our mystery guy backtracked and disappeared around the corner. I ran after him, passing Mel on my way to the corner. By the time I got to the far corner he was nowhere in sight.

When I got back to Mel, she gave me a funny look and asked "Why did you run past me?"

"You didn't even know you were being followed, did you,

Mel?"

"Yeah, I knew."

"Then why on earth did you stop here to look in your purse?"

She held up a magic marker. "Found it."

"And what were you planning to do with it, draw graffiti on him?"

"No, silly, I need it for the map."

The fact that she had a magic marker in her purse, and had chosen that moment to search her purse for it, was a little strange, even for Mel. When we got back to our apartment, Mel took her new map to the kitchen and spread it out on the table. I put a chair next to one of the living room windows overlooking the street and held back the curtains so I could watch for Rick's car. I soon got impatient and went to see how Mel was doing.

At first, when I asked her if she'd had any luck, she said, "This map wasn't much help either," then her whole demeanor changed in an instant, like a kid who's just spotted the presents under the Christmas tree. "Let's drive out there tomorrow."

I said, "You're kidding," but I knew she wasn't.

I wasn't thrilled about driving through a deserted rural area looking for a crime scene. Assuming that Reed was telling the truth, and we actually found the place, if anyone was home, they weren't likely to give us a warm reception. On the other hand, if I didn't go with her, she'd almost certainly go by herself, and that would be so much worse.

I went back into the living room and laid down on the couch to rest my feet. About ten minutes later, just as I was drifting off, I heard the front door open downstairs. Going out into the hallway, I waited for Rick and Ginger at the top of the stairs.

Rick came in first then stepped aside to let Ginger pass, no doubt he wanted to follow her up the stairs because she had on a short skirt. Strippers tend to be plain-looking at best, especially in small towns like Ithaca, but that wasn't the case with Ginger. She made the short skirt, white blouse, and strappy, high-heeled shoes she was wearing look like the pinnacle of fashion. From a staircase away, the woman looked positively stunning.

As she came closer all that changed. Her body, what I could see of it, which was quite a lot, rated a ten out of ten. But compared to my first impression of her, the close-up disappointed. I'm no fashionista, but her makeup was poorly applied, even by my lax standards. Too much and too garish, it looked as though it had been applied by someone who held a grudge against her.

Of course, she worked at the Tender Loin where the audience didn't give a hoot about her face. But she'd have to work on her makeup technique if she wanted to do more with her life than take her clothes off in front of strangers.

To be fair, Ginger did have some pluses. Her red hair was long, and wavy, and lustrous. And one of her light-brown eyes had an arresting tiny red spot beside the iris that was a real eye catcher. Of course, she didn't deserve credit for her great figure, only for keeping it up, but she had done a good job of that.

Rick wasn't at all shy about eyeing her, and I had to admit there was an excess of great looking leg showing below her dangerously short, impossibly tight skirt. My eyes would have lingered on her legs if they hadn't been drawn away by her indecent display of cleavage, a result of leaving two buttons unbuttoned that shouldn't have been. Mel would insist that Ginger's clothing left too much Ginger showing. Rick vehemently disagree with Mel's assessment, and so would I if I was honest and suicidal.

The suitcase she held tightly, as though it contained things of great value, was not much larger than a makeup case. I assumed it contained all of her worldly possessions, which in Ginger' case probably included very little of value. Of course, she wouldn't need a very big suitcase if all of her clothes were as scanty as her skirt. The suitcase meant that she had travel plans, which made me wonder what Rick had promised her. I led her and Rick into the kitchen where Mel had her map spread out on the table.

I checked the refrigerator. "I have beer and wine, and I can make coffee. Any takers?"

I was stunned when Ginger, who barely had two dimes to rub together, asked, "Is that the best you can do?"

Even if we had had something better, I wouldn't have given it to her after that remark. To placate her I searched the cupboards, coming across an almost empty bottle of cheap brandy. I poured it into a child's juice glass. As I handed it to her I asked her if Arthur Eams was with her the night his wife was killed.

She drank the brandy down like iced tea. Then, after saying she was in danger just for talking to me, she wandered into the living room as though the conversation had ended.

I got a beer out of the fridge for Rick and followed her. Mel took a seat near the window, her lips pressed together tightly as she stared at the ceiling looking very annoyed. Rick stood in the doorway, leaning on the doorjamb, sipping his beer. I sat in a chair just inside the room to the left. Ginger walked slowly along a wall of bookshelves, stopping at random to pull a book off the shelf and glance at it before putting it back in a different location.

I used my sternest courtroom voice on her. "Ginger I need to know what time Arthur got there and what time he left."

Ginger dragged a finger absently across the spines of a dozen books. "Did you read all of these?"

I told her she needed to stay focused. She spun around and looked at me blankly. I tried again. "What time did Arthur get to the club?"

She turned around to face the books again. "He always gets there early."

"And early would be what time?"

"Before I finished dancing for the day."

A dog will hang on your every word and a cat will ignore your every word, so you pretty well know where you stand with your pets. But like a moth buzzing around a light bulb after dark, my conversation with Ginger wasn't getting anywhere. But like the moth, I wasn't about to give up. "Ginger I need the time in hours and minutes."

"Yeah, okay, don't have a kitten. I try to finish up at eleven, but Struthers gets mad if he catches me staring at the clock while I'm dancing."

"So you stopped dancing at around eleven o'clock and Arthur was already there. Have I got that right?"

She took a paperback copy of *To Kill a Mockingbird* off the shelf and began flipping through the pages. "Isn't that what I just said?"

I asked her how long Arthur stayed.

"Most of the night."

"What time did he leave?"

"I didn't look at the clock"

"Was it daylight?"

"Yeah."

"Where was the sun?"

"In the sky, of course."

"Was it on the horizon?"

"No, it was higher than that, but not all the way up."

I moved on to a new topic. "Do your clients usually stay all night?"

"You said clients."

"The men who arrange to spend time with you, do they usually stay all night?

"They would if I let them."

Mel, who I didn't think was still even listening, said, "No doubt that's due to the deep intellectual connections you forge with them."

While Ginger was glaring at Mel and Mel was smiling back defiantly, I asked Ginger. "Did Arthur pay you for the whole night?"

The last thing I expected her to say was, "Arthur doesn't pay for it."

I asked her to explain that.

"What I said. Arthur gets it for free."

There had to be an interesting back story to that arrangement. "And how often does Arthur stay all night?"

"Once or twice a week."

I asked her who Struthers was.

"He runs the place."

"And why," I asked, "doesn't Arthur pay for your services when he stays overnight?"

She snickered, said, "Services, you called it services. You need to get your terms right. They're Johns. They pay for sex not services."

"Don't you ever wonder why Arthur doesn't have to pay?"

She shook her head. "Asking questions is dangerous."

"Was Arthur ever out of your sight any time that night?"

Ginger, who'd been reading, or maybe just pretending to read the jacket of a book she'd taken off the shelf, shot me a look as sharp as a piece of broken glass. "You think I enjoy being with that disgusting, fat pig?"

Like a psychologically damaged child, her emotions had flared up explosively. The very possibility that Ginger's childlike persona was part of the attraction for Arthur was disturbing. I forced those thoughts out of my mind. When her anger subsided I asked her again, "Was he with you all night? And if he did leave, how long was he gone?"

"He's old. He pees three or four times a night, but he's never gone long. Believe me, I wish he was."

"What's 'long', Ginger? Five minutes? Ten minutes?"

The grin I saw on her lips was faint, but definite. "You know how long it takes an old man to pee."

When my books no longer held her interest, she moved to the couch, slouching down into the cushions, which caused her already very short skirt to ride up. I had no doubt she knew how much leg she had showing, and no doubt it was a calculated attempt to gain an advantage over me. I asked her who she was afraid of.

While she studied her fingernails, as though the answer was written in her gaudy blue nail polish, she muttered a distracted, "What?"

I asked her again who she was afraid of.

"Struthers."

"Why are you afraid of him?"

"He runs the club."

I seemed to be hovering around another light bulb. "There must be more to it than that."

She put her hands on her hips, in an unconvincing display of anger. "Rick told me you wanted to know about Arthur. I told you about him. So you got what you wanted. Now I want some money so I can get out of this shitty little town. You owe me that."

She walked over to a radio I keep on one of my bookshelves and turned it on. After flipping past several stations she stopped on one playing a slow, sensual instrumental. With her eyes closed, she swayed in place, moving as softly as a silk dress hanging on a clothesline in a gentle breeze.

I suspected that she knew a lot more than she'd let on, but I didn't know where to dig, or the magic word that would open the door. I accused her of holding out on us and told her it would go better for her if she opened up.

Rick announced that he was going outside to check around. Ginger stopped dancing immediately, the muscles in her arms and legs tensing visibly as she watched him leave. I told her she was safe with us.

She went back to the couch. This time when she slouched her skirt rode up so high it no longer performed the function it was designed for. I told Ginger I'd be right back and went to get a beer from the kitchen. When I rejoined them I made a show of popping the tab and taking a sip. The beer had just been an excuse to leave the room so when I came back I could sit somewhere that didn't afford me such an advantageous view of Ginger.

By then I was torn between trying to get more information out of Ginger and getting her out of the apartment while Mel was still talking to me. I gave it one last shot, asking

Ginger, "So why run away now? What changed?"

"Kinda slow for a lawyer aren't you, Mr. Lee? Well, you can think about it while you pour me another drink."

She'd already had the last of the brandy, and even if I could find something else for her to drink, she hadn't earned it. "No more drinks until you tell us the rest of what you know."

She looked at me, eye to eye. "Arthur was with me when they killed his wife. Is that what you want? Are you happy now?"

"So, Ginger, might anyone else have seen Arthur at the club that night?"

"Sure, but they'd be too scared to talk about it."

Rick was going to check on that for me anyway, so I tried another topic. "What's the connection between Struthers and Arthur?"

"You know, Mr. Lee, if something happened to you, it'd be all over the news. But if something bad happens to me, they'll just say I had it coming."

She was right. If she stayed and testified, no one would thank her for it. And if something happened to her, no one would waste any time over it. She was more alone than any of us had ever been, and that made me feel bad for what I was about to do, but I thought that making her angry would help Mel get a read on her. "You're just telling me what you think I want to hear so I'll give you money."

Ginger took the bait, looking at me askance. "You calling me a liar?"

I heard a noise downstairs. I knew Ginger had heard it too because she looked at me as though she expected me to go check on it. I told her to stay put and went downstairs. Rick had come in the back door. I caught up with him downstairs, told him I wanted to talk to him before we went back up.

He grinned. "You dog, you want me to fix you up with Ginger, don't you?"

With Risk you could never be sure if he meant something. I ignored the comment. "I suspect Ginger's already told me as much as she's going to, and Mel doesn't like having her here, so let's get her on her way."

"She gets a little flaky when she needs a fix, but you gotta admit that she's easy on the eyes." He grabbed my arm when I started to go back upstairs. "One thing before we go up."

I told him that I'd had enough bad news for one day.

"So you don't want to know about the two guys sitting in a car across the street?"

"You're serious?"

"Maybe it's nothing, but I remember seeing them park there when Ginger and I were crossing the street to your apartment. And their interest in your upstairs windows seems more than casual."

"Odd coincidence," I said.

"What's that supposed to mean?"

"Someone was following Mel earlier this evening."

Then I remembered Mel and Ginger were alone together upstairs, which was more frightening than two guys parked across the street watching the house. I went up to check on them.

CHAPTER XIII

Back upstairs, I leaned into the living room and signaled for Mel to join me in the stairwell. After closing the door so Ginger wouldn't overhear us, I asked Mel what she thought of her.

"She draws attention to the parts of her body that give her the kind of reaction she craves from men. I'd be willing to bet that the body parts serving her so well now drew the attention of the wrong kind of men when she was an impressionable young girl. Unfortunately, attention of any kind can be like a drug to a misguided young girl, and that's not something good parenting can overcome."

"Anything else?"

"I'll bet you were too busy looking at her legs to notice how rarely she made eye contact with you."

"So, you think she's lying?"

"Or holding something back."

When I asked her if she was sure, she shrugged her shoulders. "It's not an exact science, Andy."

"Well, we need to get her someplace safe."

Mel's jaw dropped in an exaggerated, cartoon-like look of disbelief. "Don't tell me you bought that bullshit about something happening to her?"

"Not entirely. But Rick spotted two guys in a car across the street. They've been watching our place for a while. Could just be a coincidence, but better safe than sorry."

"One of the things I love about you, Andy, is the soft spot

you have for lowlifes in a jam. Of course, the soft spot is your head."

"That's why I keep you around, Mel - to feed my ego."

"Whatever happened in Ginger's life to get her to this place was not your fault, Andy, and nothing you do is going to fix her. Her welfare is not your responsibility."

"I'm not planning to adopt her, Mel. I just don't feel right dumping her on the street. She'd be in some jeopardy if her boss found out she was here talking to me.

"Does this have anything to do with what happened to Reed?

I shook my head.

"Well, I hope not, Andy, because that wasn't your fault. And being overprotective of Ginger won't undo what happened to him."

"I don't want to read about her in tomorrow's newspaper."

Apparently that got her hair in a bit of knot because she said, "Dean threatens us and you want to help Ginger. "Tell me, Andy, who's going to look out for us while you're looking out for everybody else?"

Mel had a point, but I still felt an obligation to do something about Ginger. I left Mel to stew about it while I went to find Ginger. She was in the living room gnawing on a piece of gum with such force it sounded as though little firecrackers were going off in her mouth. She asked me what I planned to do about about the two guys across the street.

I had an idea but I didn't have the details worked out. "You're gonna disappear tonight."

"Yeah? Where?"

"It'll be someplace where those guys, whoever they are, can't find you. That goes for Struthers and his goons too."

I found Mel in the kitchen, told her, "I think I know what to do with Ginger."

"I know what to do with her."

"Now, Mel."

She gave my hand a squeeze, told me I was losing my sense

of humor then asked me what I had planned.

"I need to line up some help. I'm going downstairs to call George. When I had gone back upstairs after the call, I asked Rick to join me in the kitchen. Ginger followed him. Mel was still there.

I told Rick to drive to the Cass Park Marina and wait for us there. He left then. We left a few minutes later. At the back door, I told Mel and Ginger to wait inside for me while I got the car. I backed it as close to the house as I could. Mel, who came out first, went straight for the front passenger seat.

Standing in the driveway holding her suitcase in her right hand, Ginger put her left hand on her hip. Still chewing her gum so forcefully it sounded like someone walking on egg shells, she said, "I don't like sitting in the back seat."

When Mel told her she could sit down right there in the driveway, Ginger muttered something under her breath, but got in the back. I turned north onto Aurora Street and headed for Salty Sam's, a popular nightclub on Ithaca's north side.

Located where the four-lane crosses a canal running south through Ithaca from Cayuga Lake, the place is a popular destination for boaters because they can tie up their boats there for dinner and drinks. On the way we were paced by a car about half a block behind us, no doubt the same car that had been parked across the street from out apartment.

Ginger stopped chewing her gum long enough to fling an insult at me. "You drive like my grandmother."

I told her the gum chewing bothered me. She asked me if I could make it any easier for someone following us. At the next corner I pulled over to the curb and stopped, partly to irritate her, and partly to see if the car behind us would pass us. It did. Moments later the taillights disappeared. I assumed they had pulled over and turned their lights off.

I spun around in my seat so I could see Ginger's reaction when I asked her, "You know who those guys are?"

She shrugged her shoulders, said, "I didn't get a good look at them," but she had that super attentive, eyes darting around, look of someone who expected trouble. Except for the sound of Ginger masticating her gum, the three of us rode the rest of the way in silence.

Salty Sam's came into view as soon as we turned onto Dey Street. The one-story building on the water's edge had been built on stilts and projected out into the canal with a boat pier running along the length of it. I pulled into the parking lot, stopping near the front door to let Mel and Ginger out.

As she was getting out of the car, Ginger told me, "I hope you know what you're doing."

I parked and went inside. The name, Salty Sam's, give no hint of the ski lodge décor of clear-finished pine posts, siding, and floors. The serious drinkers, and the not-so-serious drinkers hoping to meet someone, milled around a semi-circular pine bar thirty or forty feet in diameter near the entrance.

In the center of the room, which had been left open for dancing, a dozen or so brave couples moved more or less in time with music supplied by a live band that seemed about as enthusiastic as kids in an algebra class. A double row of tables lined the perimeter of the big open room, nearly all of them occupied by groups of rowdy young people. The place smelled of fresh beer, spilled beer, fried food, cigarettes, and ash trays.

I skirted the crowd at the bar then threaded my way through the dancers to join Mel and Ginger who were waiting for me on the far side of the room.

Mel nodded toward the entrance. "Two guys came in behind you. They're standing by the front door. They're definitely looking for someone."

I glanced at them then turned away. There was no mistaking Jack, the big muscular man from the Tender Loin, and Nate, his shorter heavy set partner. No doubt they were looking for Ginger. And it wouldn't go well for Mel and me if we got in their way. "Time for us to leave," I said, gesturing to the back door.

That got me a scowl and an angry-sounding, "That's it? That's your whole plan, Einstein?" from Ginger.

Once outside, I directed them to a blue-hulled Bowrider motorboat. As Mel and Ginger climbed in, I took the mooring rope off the deck cleat and pushed the boat away from the dock with my foot.

Jack and Nate came through the door. I yelled to George to get us out of there. He fired up the outboard. Jack looked our way. George slammed the throttled to full power. The boat churned water, Jack ran toward us, coming fast with Nate at his heels. The boat surged forward, away from the dock. Jack stopped then Nate. They stood on the pier glaring at us.

George tossed life jackets at us. We were several hundred feet from the pier, and well into the channel, before he pulled back on the throttle enough for us to talk. "Well, that was exciting," he said, displaying a big toothy smile. An old and trusted friend, George's high forehead separated his close-cropped hair from the boyish face that was home to an ever-present smile. Always upbeat, even when he didn't have a right to be; always trying to cheer me up, even when I didn't need to be; his good nature could be overwhelming at times. But when I was in a tough spot and needed someone reliable, I called George.

I handed him a wad of twenty dollar bills for the gas and for giving up his evening to help us out. "Take us to Cass Park, George."

"What's that?" Ginger asked, scowling at me.

"That's where Rick's waiting to pick up Mel and me. You stay with George. He'll take you up the lake to his cottage. From there he'll drive you to Auburn where you can catch a bus."

I gave her three hundred dollars half expecting her to give me some grief about the amount, but she just looked off into the distance. Rick had suggested that I give her two hundred, but then he can be a cheapskate.

George throttled up again, taking us out of the calm channel into the much choppier water of Cayuga Lake. The outboard motor and the slap of the water against the hull made talk impossible. Luckily, it was a short trip to another channel, one that runs south from the lake through the west end of

Ithaca. After the rough lake, a slow ride in the calm water of the channel was a welcome relief.

George pulled the boat up to a dock at the Cass Park Marina where Rick was waiting for us. He came and held the boat for Mel and me while we climbed out. George smiled and waved as he turned the boat around to head back up the channel toward the open lake.

Rick dropped Mel and me off in Salty Sam's parking lot to get our car. When we got home I suggested to Mel that we have a glass of wine.

"Any other night, Andy. But right now I'd like a shower."

"I sometimes feel that way after a day of dealing with lowlifes."

"If by lowlife, you mean Ginger, then I agree."

I lay on the couch sipping a glass of wine while I waited for my turn in the shower. Even though it was an expensive wine I didn't much care for it. For me, the better the wine, the less likely I am to like it. Mel was the wine connoisseur. She also enjoyed taking long, hot, soothing showers, which is what she did that night.

When I came out of the bathroom after my shower, I found Mel curled up in bed with the covers pulled over her head. I could tell from her shallow, steady breathing that she was sound asleep. I had felt exhausted and drowsy before my shower. After my shower I felt exhausted and wide awake. It left my mind free to dwell on all of the disappointments of the previous two days. Unfortunately, I didn't expect the next several days to be much better.

I wondered if sending Ginger away had been a mistake. If I didn't come up with anything else, her testimony would be Arthur's only chance to stay out of prison. To add to my distress, Mel was determined to look for that cabin in the morning. To say she's tenacious is like saying the winters in Ithaca are long and cold.

CHAPTER XIV

Mel got me up so early Wednesday morning to look for the cabin that it was still dark when we left. It can get pretty cool here at night in the early fall, especially when it's as clear as it was that morning. The first hard frost had to be just around the corner.

I usually do the driving, but that morning, as we were getting in the car, she said something along the lines of, "You can't drive in that condition."

"That's what you tell a drunk, Mel."

"Stop complaining and start navigating."

After a glance at the map I told her to take Spencer Road.

"I already knew that."

After taking several measurements on the map with my finger I told Mel, "A ruler would've improved our chances of knowing where we are."

"You mean it would've improved your chances of knowing where we are."

I told her to take Stone Quarry Road up South hill.

"I already knew that."

We drove past the hulking, dark shapes of boarded-up buildings, remnants of businesses that had made a few people wealthy and left a lot of other people feeling betrayed. Glaring security lights shone on deserted parking lots where weeds sprouted through the crumbling pavement.

Seeing those reminders of my hometown's declining fortunes troubled me. "It's hard to believe now, Mel, but so many people worked in this area when I was kid that the roads were choked with traffic when the factories let out."

We passed a small oil storage depot on the left and a series of light industrial businesses on the right. Most of the road was lined on both sides with chain-link fencing, some of it topped with coiled razor wire, a nightmare version of a Slinky toy. On many of the buildings, rusted, corrugated sheet metal served as both the siding and the roofing, and plywood, so discolored from dirt and water stains that it resembled Op Art, had replaced most of the window glass.

Mel wasn't a local girl. I assumed that's why she didn't seem upset by it all. I asked her how long she thought it would take to turn the decay around.

"If that's not a rhetorical question, it should be, so I'm not gonna answer it. And don't let it get to you, Hon, because it'll never again be the way it was when you were a kid."

Then she turned on the radio - discussion over. Short song clips and bursts of static grated on my nerves while she searched for a station. "You know, Andy, maybe it hasn't really changed."

"Mel, I can see the changes."

"Back then, you were looking at Ithaca through a kid's eyes. Maybe you just didn't see the decay."

We soon passed a thin, forlorn-looking man walking along the side of the road, his collar turned up against the cold, damp morning air blowing at him, and the cold indifferent world surrounding him. I turned around to watch him as his image faded into the morning mist. "What kind of life do you suppose he has, to be walking along such a desolate stretch of road at this hour?"

I looked over at Mel, caught her rolling her eyes. "The kind of life you have when the only nourishment you get comes from a bottle in a brown bag."

I asked her if she was trying to cheer me up.

"Honestly, Andy, I think you feel sorry for everybody."

As the early morning sun came up over East Hill, a wave of yellow light swept silently down West Hill, making our surroundings look even drearier. My attention was drawn back to the roadside by a jolt from a pothole and the acrid smell of machine oil. I thought I could actually feel the lubricant when I rubbed my fingers together.

I made the mistake of saying, "The only green I saw on that whole ugly stretch was a few dusty weeds on the side of the road."

"What's gotten into you, Andy?

"I didn't have any coffee or breakfast before we left."

"I'm your wife, Andy, not your mother. You could've gotten up in time to make coffee, and breakfast too. But you chose to sleep instead. So, stow the complaints until we get back."

Mel had turned onto Stone Quarry Road which winds up the west side of South Hill. Steep even by Ithaca's standards, it's a winding narrow road with no shoulders that's especially dangerous when it's icy. But coming down the hill into town at night, in the winter, when the trees have shed their leaves, the ride affords you a magnificent panoramic view of Ithaca and Cornell.

When the road leveled out, swinging south along the spine of the hill, we left the soot and decay behind. A few miles farther the pavement ended and we passed into an area of mixed woods and open fields. The car was churning up a swirling cloud of dust behind us that looked like a jet's contrail.

Because the only two FM stations in the area were associated with the colleges, they played music that appealed mostly to young people. So Mel had settled on an AM station playing top ten songs. When the deejay played a Barry Manilow song, Mel turned the radio off, twisting the knob hard, as though she wanted to punish the radio for playing the song. As we passed into an area of dense undergrowth Mel made a comment about the trees looking small and sickly.

"It's new growth," I told her, "just bushes and scrub trees, the kind of place rabbits like because predators won't go in after them. Whoever put up the 'posted' signs had a sense of humor, because that hedge row is tighter than a preacher's ass."

"Thanks for the image, Andy, I'll cherish it."

"You know, Mel, I read somewhere that the forests around here offered the early settlers magnificent vistas because the canopies were so high and dense that there was very little undergrowth to block their view."

She told me I was a fount of useless information then asked me, "How much farther?"

"We should come to a 'T' pretty soon. That'll be Halsey Road, and as near as I can tell from this map, we're more likely to find a hunting cabin if we go left, but that's just a guess."

We passed a small farm about a quarter of a mile after turning onto Halsey. The farm house, a typical nondescript little country place, didn't fit any particular architectural style, and judging from the peeling paint and numerous roof patches, the farm was no longer financially viable.

The farm fields abruptly became dense forest as the road dropped into a gorge, gently at first, then becoming steeper until the road became a switchback path, descending into the gloom of the narrow valley below. Each time we rounded a curve, our tires lost purchase in the gravel and we slide precariously close to the ditch.

A few minutes later we passed a turnoff. Mel tried to stop. The car slid past it. She backed up then turned into a driveway barely wide enough for the car. Dark and overgrown, the place felt claustrophobic and threatening.

"You do realize, Mel, that this is private property, right?"

"We'll just say we were looking for a friend's place and got the wrong driveway."

"I hope Dean's associates buy that if we run into them."

The driveway was so badly rutted, the car rocked like a boat in rough water, its springs squealing like a wounded animal. Then, without warning, the woods opened into a clearing. We came to a stop with our headlights shining on the windows of a house trailer; so much for being subtle. I surveyed the site as I waited nervously for signs of life. I had no real desire to meet the owners.

Plastic tarps, held down by old car tires, covered the roof of the trailer. The faded paint job, the rusty trim, and the rounded corners of the roof, were all signs that it was a very old trailer in a low rent district.

Had I been fully awake, I would've known what to expect from Mel, and might've been quick enough to stop her before she got out of the car. Instead, I watched her walk over to the trailer and peer into several of the windows before coming back to the car.

"Mel, that wasn't smart. To start with, we're trespassing. And what if you'd come face to face with one of Dean's buddies?"

"But I didn't," she said, as though that made it okay.

How could I possibly argue with that logic? She got us back out to the road and headed downhill. After the next bend, Mel slowed down opposite a small ranch house perched across the slope of the hill. It had a narrow perimeter of yard around it where the woods had been cut back. Mel got out of the car to check on the house. I got out of the car to keep an eye on Mel.

She knocked on the front door, but the effort was half-hearted and she didn't wait long enough for anyone to answer before she walked over to the big picture window and peered in with her hands cupped around her face.

Her next stop was the detached garage behind the house. She rubbed her sleeve on one of the windows and looked in. I couldn't talk her out of lifting the garage door to look inside. So much for keeping her out of trouble. It was classic Mel. I asked her to be more careful. She poked her lower lip out. She didn't take scolding well.

"Mel, please don't open any more doors."

"But the window was so filthy I couldn't see in."

On our way back to the car, I told her that dirty windows didn't make opening doors legal. She ignored me. After she got us headed downhill again she said, "Believe it or not, that place actually looked clean inside. I can't see somebody like Dean being that neat."

"Mel, you can't equate messiness with criminality."

She gave me warning look. I knew she thought there was a correlation. We also passed the next driveway before the car slid to a stop, so Mel had to back up. Riding with Mel when she's backing up is an adventure because she overcompensates every time she turns the wheel, tracing a snake's path. I asked her to stop the car.

She stopped the car, but based on the look she gave me, I hadn't scored any points with her. "You're going to drive me nuts, Andy."

I asked her to let me drive.

She slumped forward, resting her forehead on the steering wheel. "Now what?" she asked.

If there's a cabin in there, and anyone's home, they could be associates of Dean."

"So?"

"So, they could be dangerous. I might not be able to protect you."

"I appreciate your concern, Andy, but what's that got to do with my driving?"

"What if this is the place, Mel, and we have to leave in a hurry? What if there isn't enough room for you to turn the car around?"

"Yeah, yeah, okay," she said, "you made your point. Don't make a federal case out of it."

We traded places. I followed the driveway deep into the woods. It ended at a one-car detached garage with a severe westerly slant and a cabin beyond that. The wild grass growing around the garage and cabin where the woods had been cut back, looked dry and dead. Brush and weeds had grown around and up through a pile of unrecognizable rusty metal on the far edge of the clearing.

A jacked-up, blue, four-wheel-drive pickup truck like the one I'd seen near the D&P warehouse was parked in front of the garage. We'd found the cabin. I shifted the car into reverse. I backed up as fast as I dared, not nearly as fast as I wanted.

Mel asked me why we were leaving, and "What's the rush?"

"This is the place."

"How do you know?"

"Because I saw that same truck parked near the warehouse the night Reed was killed. And you can bet that whoever's in there is no Sunday school teacher."

"Are you sure?"

"How could I mistake a truck like that?"

"No, silly, I meant, how can you be sure he's not a Sunday school teacher?"

"Really, Mel?"

She giggled like a school girl.

Out of the driveway and retracing our route back up the hill, I couldn't get the car going fast enough to suit me but every time I gave it more gas it lost traction.

As we crested the hill, I said, "This was probably a bad idea, Mel."

She told me I was overreacting.

"If it was Dean's accomplice who opened the curtains and we spooked him, he might get rid of any evidence that would prove Sara was there."

Mel giggled. "We spook him and he cleans house. What is he, gay?"

"You need to take this seriously, Mel."

"And you forgot your survival training."

"What are you talking about?"

"What'd I teach you about survival, Andy?"

"That you're always right?"

"And yet you argue with me."

I asked her if she got a good look at the guy in the window.

"No."

We had crested the hill and were soon passing through open fields again. Dewdrops clinging to the field grass caught the low morning sun, creating thousands of tiny, sparkling rainbows. After checking to be sure there were no cars in sight behind us, I pulled over to enjoy the spectacle. Sadly, it began to fade when as soon as we got out of the car. `

By the time we reached the hill above Ithaca, the rumbling protestations of my empty stomach were too much to ignore. I asked Mel if she wanted to stop for breakfast.

"I'd have to change first."

"Change what?"

"I can't possibly go anywhere dressed like this."

"But, Mel, you wore that same outfit to dinner last week."

"After all the time we've been together, you still don't get it, do you, Andy."

When we got home, I couldn't talk her out of changing her clothes before we ate. While she was occupied with that, I scrambled half a dozen eggs, cooked three slices of toast, and half a pound of bacon. I have to say that the eggs, filled with grated cheese, diced peppers, onion flakes, and oregano, didn't taste half bad.

Mel told me later that I needed supervision when I cooked, no doubt a reference to the quantity of bacon. And yet, between us we finished almost everything. Half an hour later, while washing the dishes, I caught myself wondering what Mrs. Jennings was hiding and why. When I gave up on that, I tried to make sense of Dean's case. That left me wondering what Ginger was hiding and why.

What I needed was an informant to come out of the woodwork and hand me information that would break things wide open. That rarely happens, and never twice in the same case. For the Dean case, it had been Reed. Unfortunately, he was dead. For the Eams case it should have been Ginger, but I'd sent her away.

Before I left the house I called Anne to tell her I'd need the next couple of days open and asked her to reschedule all of my appointments.

CHAPTER XV

My car was scheduled for maintenance that day. We dropped it off at the dealer's. Mel dropped me off at the courthouse. When she pulled over to the curb to let me out, she announced that we had to go back to the cabin.

Disbelief hardly described what I felt. "You didn't hear anything I said this morning, did you?"

"I did too. You said we might have spooked them. That's why we have to do it tonight."

I said the only thing I could think of, "Absolutely not."

She waited until I'd gotten out and my door was almost closed before saying, "We'll go after dark," then sped away before I could argue.

A breeze rustled the leaves in the walnut trees lining the courthouse sidewalk. Somewhere above me an angry squirrel scolded me for walking under his tree. Then a cloud passed in front of the sun, dropping the air temperature ten degrees, a portent that autumn rains and cold north winds would soon descend upon Central New York.

Clouds arrive here sometime in late October, creating an oppressive gray gloom that can linger until April with few breaks. And those breaks come when the temperature drops so low that the snow being compressed by your shoes sounds like the creaking leather of a horse's saddle. Those days are crisp and clear. The thought of facing another long, cold, Ithaca winter darkened my already gloomy outlook.

Rose of Sharon bushes lined the front of the courthouse.

All of their purple flower petals had long since fallen blanketing the ground around them. Every time I passed them I resolved to plant some at home where Mel and I could see them while we drink our morning coffee.

The marble walls and floor of the courthouse lobby echoed even the faintest of conversations, making it sound as though twice as many people were passing through its halls. It got me wondering how many people had walked those corridors; so many that their shoes had worn hollows in the marble stair treads.

I took the stairs down to the records office in the basement and asked the clerk for the transcript of Dean's trial from sixteen years earlier. I couldn't help wondering if the wooden chairs in the waiting area, which were too small to be comfortable, and the wooden desks, which were too small to be useful, were intended to discourage lengthy stays.

A pleasant-looking young woman brought me the file. It was a quick read. According to the testimony of a police officer, they'd learned of Herb's murder when his body was discovered by a hiker several days after the fact.

Apparently Dean had told a local dancer named Cherry that he planned to rob the guy. Maybe Dean was just a dim-witted felon after all. There was some circumstantial evidence, but his conviction had been based mostly on the dancer's testimony. During cross examination the defense made the most of her occupation as a dancer, aka stripper, insinuating that she was a drug addict and therefore an unreliable witness. Apparently she was convincing. At eleven o'clock I returned the transcript to the clerk and headed for my office. I wanted to check in with Anne before she left for lunch.

Anne looked surprised, but not particularly happy, to see me. "It wasn't easy," she said, "but I rescheduled all of your appointments for the rest of this week."

"I'm sorry, Anne, but things will be hectic for a while. I need you to let me know if anything comes up that I can't let slide."

"You just missed a call from Rick. He said it was important, and that you could find him at the library. And Arthur Eams called twice, once late yesterday afternoon, and then again early this morning."

I told her I'd call Arthur before I left to meet Rick and asked her if there was anything else.

She handed me a several slips of paper with names and phone numbers on them. "These will all keep."

"Thanks Anne. I should be back this afternoon. But if someone asks for me, and it's not someone you know, tell them you don't know when I'll be back."

That surprised her. "Are you in some kind of trouble, Andy?"

I assured her that everything was fine and went to my office to call Arthur. I got lucky. He'd just stepped out. His secretary switched me over to his answering machine. I told him I didn't have any news for him, that I'd give him an update Friday, and to leave a message with Anne if he had anything he needed to tell me. After that, I headed for the library to find Rick.

Located on the corner of Cayuga and Tioga Streets, it was housed in a building originally used by Ithaca College for classes. I found Rick downstairs sitting at one of the microfiche machines.

"Over here, Andy," he said, as he spun the dial causing the screen to become a blur.

He played with the dial until an image settled on the screen. Then he got up and told me to sit where he'd been sitting. He tapped the screen. "That's your buddy Dean."

A newspaper photo of a young looking Ronnie Dean being led into a courtroom filled the screen on the viewer. I checked the date. It was a sixteen year old newspaper. I told him I already knew about the original trial, that I'd read the transcript earlier that morning.

"There's more," he said, spinning the dial, going forward in time.

He stopped the display on a page of short articles and

103

pointed to one of them. "There, read that."

It took me less than a minute to get through it. "So Dean said he was framed. They all say that."

This time, Rick moved the wheel carefully to the next day's front page, which featured a large photograph in the top center of the page showing a crowd leaving the courthouse.

I asked him what I was looking at.

"It's right there in front of you, boss."

"Do me a favor. Pretend I'm a little slow and tell me what I should see."

He tapped the screen with his index finger. "Take a good look at that woman. Imagine her with long hair."

"Sorry, Rick, but I'm not coming up with anything."

"Tell me she doesn't look like Sara."

"How do you know what Sara looks like?"

"Hey, give me some credit, will ya? That's what you pay me for."

He tapped on the screen again. "That's Sara's mother. I'd put money on it."

"Sorry, Rick, I just don't see the resemblance."

"In the article they give her name as Cherry, but that'll be her stage name. And according to this, it was Cherry's testimony that got Dean convicted. Think what that would mean if it was Jennings."

I pushed the chair back from the viewer. "If Cherry is Jennings, it explains why Dean attacked her."

"Not bad, huh Boss?"

"Except that you're supposed to be working for me, not Francis. This would help him convict Dean."

"You want the truth, or don't you?"

"Well, if it helps to put Dean behind bars where he belongs that's a good thing. But it also puts me in an awkward spot. No matter how much I want Dean back in prison, he is my client. The judge would frown on it if I helped Francis convict him. So for now, this will have to be our secret."

Rick took the fiche slide out and turned off the viewer. "I'm right about this, Andy. I know it."

"I need to know if that is Mrs. Jennings. I'll talk to her again."

I asked him to take a walk with me so we could talk without whispering. We crossed the street to a picturesque little city park crisscrossed with tree-lined sidewalks. On its north side the spire of a big, gothic-style church towered over the trees. I chose a bench with enough clear space between the pigeon droppings for both of us to sit down. Rick sat forward on the bench, resting his elbows on his knees and eyed the people walking by.

Watching him made me uncomfortable. "You're not someone who can enjoy just sitting in the park on a nice day, are you?"

"Hey," he said, "how about that detective work?"

"Yeah, remind me to give you a bonus for it someday, assuming you're right about Jennings."

"I am. You'll see."

A young couple walked by. After they had passed, he pointed a thumb at them and said, "People like Dean don't exist in their world. Sara used to feel safe too, just like them. We can't give that back to her, even if we put Dean away forever."

He was right, of course. I told him he was depressing me.

"Dealing with creeps like Dean is a slippery slope. You can't let your world look like his."

"Meaning?"

"You're an idealist, Andy, hang on to that."

"I appreciate your concern, Rick, but getting back to this revelation about Mrs. Jennings, how does it help me?"

"Ithaca's a small town," he said, stopping after that one simple statement.

For a while I enjoyed a chorus of birdsong. Then my impatience got the better of me. "So Ithaca's a small town, so what?"

Rick had taken out a small pocket knife and was using it to scrape dirt out from under his fingernails. "Ithaca doesn't have a big underworld. There aren't many people in it. Some of them are visitors, like our Mayor when he gets horny. Some of them, like Ginger, drift through and are soon forgotten. A few of them live in it and off of it for long periods. Dean was one of those."

"If I was a judge, I'd ask you where you're going with this."

"Sixteen years ago Jennings was a stripper who went by the name Cherry, and her testimony sent Dean to prison. He came back for revenge. I think it's as simple as that, Andy."

"If that's true, Rick, she'll want that to stay buried. For her sake, and Sara's, so let's keep it between us. They've already had their share of misery."

"I've dug up enough dirt over the years to fill in the lake. It's an occupational hazard." He tapped the side of his head. "And I keep it up here."

Sometimes Rick's cavalier attitude made it hard to see the good guy hiding beneath the crusty exterior that shielded him from a steady diet of broken people and corruption. I told him I had something else for him. "Mel and I found a hunting cabin this morning. I think it's where Dean took Sara."

"Jesus, Andy, how'd you manage that when the police couldn't?"

"I'll let Mel tell you how. She'd like that. But for now, I want you to go to the county clerk's office and find out who owns the place."

"Is that all you've got for me?"

"I know you don't like doing that sort of thing. That's why I pay you. And speaking of research, what'd you find out about Arthur Eams' car?"

"The roof is unusual but it's not custom."

"That meant there could be more than one in town, however unlikely. Fortunately, doubt is cumulative, so every bit of uncertainty counts, no matter how insignificant. I stood up slowly, like an old man, my back stiff from not sitting properly. I told Rick to follow me.

"Where're we headed?"

"To the bookstore to buy a survey map so I can show you

106

where this cabin is."

"So," he said, "I guess I'm going to the clerk's office after all."

"When you're done with that, get us two flashlights, a pair of walkie-talkies, some extra batteries, and keep the receipts so I can expense them.

"What's all that for?"

"Mel wants to go back out there tonight, and I want you with us this time, so wear something appropriate."

"That doesn't sound like the sort of job for a couple of amateurs like you and Mel. You should stay home and look up something in one of your expensive law books, or are they just for show?"

"Mel has her mind set on going. Do you want to tell her she's can't?"

"Not unless you give me hazard pay."

I bought a copy of the survey map at the bookstore and showed him where we found the cabin. Before we left there I told him to meet us at the Pine Tavern for dinner at eight o'clock, seven if he wanted dinner, my treat.

"Then I'll see you at seven," he said as he left for the clerk's office.

I called Mrs. Jennings from a phone booth. She picked up right after her answering machine so I had to wait for the electronics to stop screeching. "Mrs. Jennings, this is Andrew Lee."

"I've got nothing to say to you, Mr. Lee."

"There's something you should know, and it'll be too late once the trial starts."

I gave her a moment to respond. She didn't. "Mrs. Jennings, I wouldn't call if it wasn't important."

"I'll come to your office tomorrow."

I didn't want Dean finding out. "That's not a good idea. Can you meet me at the Ithaca Diner?"

"When?"

"Fifteen minutes?"

I didn't like taking advantage of her grief, but I didn't feel as though I had any other options. "You need to do this for Sara."

"I'll be there in twenty."

Five minutes later I got to the Ithaca Diner, already feeling anxious about asking her questions that might open up old wounds.

CHAPTER XVI

The Ithaca Diner, located in the four hundred block of State Street, has been there as long as I can remember. I chose the place because we weren't likely to be seen there by anyone I knew. Still, to play it safe, I sat in a booth toward the back, away from the front windows.

Wearing a classy-looking light gray dress with half-a-dozen dark gray buttons down the center of it and a flowery scarf of reds and oranges, Mrs. Jennings looked as out of place as a bride in a war zone. She slid into the seat across from me. I thanked her for coming.

When she looked at me, it felt as though her eyes were boring into my head. "Tell me why I'm here, Mr. Lee?"

"It'll be a lot easier for Francis to get a conviction if Sara testifies."

"He wouldn't dare."

"He's running for re-election, Mrs. Jennings, and this case could be great publicity for him. And a little sensationalism never hurts, like having a teenage girl on the stand describing what Dean did to her."

"How can he do that? she said, as a statement, not a question, and stridently, as if saying it with enough determination would make it so.

"He can subpoena her."

"But she's a minor."

"I'm sorry," Mrs. Jennings, "but the law does allow it. And if she fails to comply, she can be held in contempt."

The moment I put my hand on hers I knew it was a mistake. She pulled it away as though my touch had burned her. She started to slide out of the booth.

I told her to call Francis and get his assurance that he wouldn't put Sara on the stand then pointed toward the back of the diner. "There's a payphone near the restrooms." I pushed a quarter and a slip of paper across the table. "That's his number. Call him. Ask him to give you his word that he won't put Sara on the stand. If he won't give you his word, come back and talk to me."

She reached over to get her purse off the seat. "I'll go see him tomorrow."

"There isn't time, Mrs. Jennings."

She looked at me in silence for what seemed an eternity before she took the quarter and the slip of paper.

She stood at the phone for several minutes. When she came back to the booth her age lines looked more pronounced, and her eyes lacked the determination I'd seen in them minutes earlier. She slumped into the seat across the table from me. That told me what I needed to know. "I'm sorry, Mrs. Jennings, but you needed to hear this before it's too late to do anything about it."

The woman sitting across from me looked disheartened and frail. I offered to get her a cup of coffee. When she didn't refuse, I flagged a waitress by holding up my cup and pointing to Mrs. Jennings.

While I did that Mrs. Jennings took a compact out of her purse and flipped it open, looking at herself in the little mirror. She fussed with her hair, tucking in a loose strand. The waitress brought her a coffee, which she stirred but didn't drink.

When I said, "Sixteen years ago, you were using the name Cherry," a muscle over her left eye twitched. I'd hit a nerve. "Your testimony put Dean in prison sixteen years ago."

She asked me a question I couldn't answer. "Why would God let him hurt my little girl?" She asked me another question before I had time to answer that one. "And why Sara? I was the one who testified against him."

I couldn't help thinking that Dean had molested Sara to make the most of his revenge. What could be more painful for a mother than for someone to hurt her child, especially if it was brought on by something she did?

"Mr. Lee, Sara can never find out about my former life, or that I know Dean. It would devastate her. If you want my cooperation, you have to assure me that won't happen."

Experience has taught me that telling the truth is usually safer than hiding it, but that can be a hard lesson. "Your secrets are safe with me, Mrs. Jennings. But if working with criminals has taught me anything, it's that your silence won't keep Sara safe."

She set her spoon down on her napkin very carefully then took a deep breath. "I was just a kid, Mr. Lee. I had no idea what those people were capable of."

She tipped her cup and stared at the coffee in it. "I was underage when I started dancing, but I was good. I had regulars who came to see me. I assumed Struthers liked me because I always drew a crowd, but he had bigger plans for me. Dancing is degrading and depressing. The drugs Struthers gave us helped, but it also made us easy to control. Pretty soon he started setting me up with men."

I think she misread my expression because she locked eyes with me again. "You have no right to judge me, Mr. Lee. You don't know anything about me or what I've been through."

"I'm not judging you, Mrs. Jennings. But I have questions I'd rather ask you here, in private, than in a courtroom. That way they can stay buried.

She nodded her assent. I asked my first question. "I doubt you're the only person responsible for putting Dean in prison, but he only went after you. Why do you think that is?"

She shrugged her shoulders, said she didn't know.

"Okay, Mrs. Jennings, we'll set that aside for now."

Sitting there silent and unmoving behind her cosmetic mask, she reminded me of one of those antique dolls with the porcelain faces. I worried she might leave without finishing her story. Fortunately there's something in the human psyche that compels us to finish the narratives we've started in our defense. Eventually she resolved whatever was holding her back and resumed her story. "One of my regular customers came to me. He promised he'd get me out of that life. All I had to do was lie to the police about Dean. I should've told him no, but I really did want out."

When I asked her for the guy's name she began rubbing her arms as though she gotten a chill, even though the place actually felt a little too warm. Then instead of answering my question she resumed her narrative where she'd left off. "I asked him what he wanted me to tell the police. I was naïve, Mr. Lee. That doesn't make me a bad person."

Once again she paused to look at me, possibly still wondering what I thought of her. "Mrs. Jennings, you have to answer to yourself, to God if you believe in him, and maybe to a jury, for what you did, but not to me." It wasn't polished but it was enough to get her talking again.

"I got worried when I didn't hear from my friend for a couple of days. Then one of the other girls told me that the club's owner had been robbed and was missing. That's when I got scared."

A young couple came in. They looked down on their luck, not wearing the best clothes, and definitely not using the Queen's English. They walked toward the back of the diner, passing by our booth. Mrs. Jennings waited until they were out of earshot before she resumed.

"My friend came to see me the next day. He told me that the police had found Herb's body, that he'd been killed."

I interrupted to ask her if Herb was the former owner.

"Yeah. Anyway, my friend told me I should so to the police and tell them that Dean had asked me when the next big drug buy was going to be, that he wanted to know when Herb would have a big load of cash on hand."

So it wasn't just Sara that Mrs. Jennings had been protecting with her silence. She had knowingly lied on the stand, and her testimony had put the wrong man in prison for sixteen years. I wondered about her life with Sara, about the lies that had been hanging over them all those years, just like the Sword of Damocles. And I wondered what would happen to their relationship if Sara ever learned the truth about her mother.

Then Mrs. Jennings pulled her hair back from the side of her head to show me a scar above her ear. She talked a little slower, as though the memories were difficult or painful. "He did this with a knife. He said that the next scar would show if I said anything to anyone.

I made a run for it when he left. Eventually a patrol car spotted me and took me to the hospital. I guess the cut looked worse than it was. The next morning a policeman came and asked me a lot of questions. I told him the lies about Dean, just like I was told to. He seemed satisfied and left, but a detective came back later."

She dabbed her eyes with a tissue. Some friend that guy turned out to be. There was something fishy about the emergency room too. The physician wouldn't have kept her in the hospital overnight just because of the cut over her ear. The doctor would have stitched it up and sent her on her way. I suspected the police of bribing or threatening the doctor to keep her there, a sort of protective custody without the need to arrest her or provide her with a lawyer.

She used the tissue to wipe her nose before continuing. "The detective told me that the police had arrested Dean for the murder. He wanted me to testify against him. He told me they'd protect me if I did, and that I'd be back on the street if I didn't. So, of course, I agreed."

I asked her if the other dancers at the club had backed up her story.

"I'm the only one who lied about Dean."

"They didn't contradict your story?"

"Dean was a real bastard to all of us girls. He often took us against our will. So no, they didn't contradict me. They were as glad to see him put away as I was."

113

"So you did talk to them?"

"I went back to work after Dean was put away."

"Your friend didn't get you out?"

"Eventually."

I asked her for the names of the women she worked with,

"They've all left town. I should've left too, but I had no money and nowhere to go. I did change my name, but they could've found me if they wanted to. You can't hide in a little place like Ithaca. Everyone must have been glad that Dean had taken the fall for the murder. Otherwise they would've come after me."

If what Mrs. Jennings had told me was true, that she was an accessory to murder, then she had a compelling reason to keep her past a secret. And I had the trigger I'd been looking for. Her false testimony had set up the chain of events that led to Dean kidnapping her daughter.

And yet I still had the feeling she was hiding something and I called her on it. "Mrs. Jennings, we can't predict what will happen if we cross someone like Dean, but we can be sure we'll pay dearly. Our only defense is to tell the truth. Then when terrible things happen, we aren't responsible for them, and we don't have to live with the guilt."

"Maybe that kind of abstract thinking works for you, Mr. Lee, but it doesn't for me. Being righteous is no consolation if something bad happens to your child."

"There's nothing abstract about it, Mrs. Jennings. Dean wanted revenge for what you did to him sixteen years ago. If we don't set things right, he'll go back to prison and brood over it again. I don't like to think about what he'll do when he gets out next time."

"I do what I have to do to protect Sara now, not years from now."

"And how old is Sara Mrs. Jennings?"

"That's got nothing to do with any of this," she said then stood up to leave."

I asked her for the name of the man who had her lie to the

police. She turned around and started to walk away.

"Mrs. Jennings, a nightmare came for you and Sara because of your complicity sixteen years ago."

She stopped but kept her back to me.

"The scales of justice will be out of balance until you tell the world what else happened back then. The payment will come due, Mrs. Jennings. You can't hide from it.

After she left, the waitress brought the check and asked me if I wanted a refill on my coffee. I declined. It wasn't good. But before I left I took a few minutes to think through what Jennings had told me. If she wouldn't give me the names of the people she'd been involved with, then I'd hit a dead end. And I couldn't have Rick dig into it because I'd promised her that her secret was safe with me.

I did think it odd that she left when I asked her old Sara was. I dug out enough cash for the two coffees and a decent tip. Overall it was money well spent.

CHAPTER XVII

I called Mel from the Diner payphone and asked her to come pick me up. I was in the mood for a break. When I got in the car Mel told me she'd checked three of the five names on the security card listing.

"And?"

"Nothing."

"That's a disappointment."

"Well, Andy, where can we go to cheer you up?"

"Taughannock Park."

"Then Taughannock Park it is."

Driving west on Buffalo Street toward the four-lane, she asked me how my day was going.

I told her about the newspaper photos Rick found from Dean's murder trial.

"And?"

"And Rick thought he spotted the Jennings woman in one of them."

"Really?"

I filled Mel in on my talk with Mrs. Jennings, giving her the facts, letting her draw her own conclusions, which she did. "She actually admitted to committing perjury that put a man in prison, albeit a not so innocent man. But still."

"I told her about how our actions can have unanticipated consequences, like Dean coming back for revenge."

"In other words, Andy, you dumped a mountain of guilt on her."

116

She had a point. It didn't make me feel any better.

A few minutes later, as we crossed the four-lane, Mel said, "If Dean is telling the truth, that he didn't molest Sara, then why'd he kidnap her?"

"That does seem a little bizarre. Maybe if we knew what else happened sixteen years ago we could figure that out."

She groaned, said in a sing-song voice, "I feel a lecture coming on."

I didn't let that keep me from making my point. "Mrs. Jennings let the horses out of the barn when she conspired with the police to put Dean in prison.

"Horses, Andy? Was that really necessary?"

"I thought it was kinda clever."

"Andy, you do realize that you're blaming the victim for what happened."

"It's not a matter of blame, Mel. It's cause and effect."

"Andy, bringing up what happened sixteen years ago isn't going to protect Jennings and her daughter from Dean."

"There's no question that Dean is a bad guy, Mel, and that he deserves to be punished. But Jennings gave false testimony that put him in prison. I understand her desperation and the choices she made, but Dean came after her and Sara because of those choices."

"She's afraid, Andy, afraid of what Dean will do to Sara if he goes free, now, this year."

"If you make someone like Dean angry, you have to live with the consequences, and the consequences can be ugly. And keeping secrets will only keep you safe for so long."

"I don't agree, Andy. She was a foolish young girl when she sent Dean to prison. Doing the right thing now won't fix that."

"We should always take the high road, Mel. Then, if something goes wrong, it's not on our balance sheet. I can't imagine the guilt Mrs. Jennings feels knowing she could have prevented what happened to her daughter. And yet the woman is still holding something back."

"You're not going to let this rest, are you, Andy? Not until you know what everybody had for breakfast sixteen years ago."

"Dean paying an arbitrary price for his crimes is hardly what I'd call justice, Mel. And, if Dean wasn't guilty of the murder, then there's been a killer on the loose for sixteen years, and that's outside my comfort level."

"Point taken, if you're right about having a killer on the loose."

We followed Taughannock Boulevard north out of Ithaca. The road cuts through dense woods along the west side of Cayuga Lake, occasionally affording a glimpse of the lake through a break in the trees, and rising as much as a hundred feet above the cottages lining the west shore of the lake; cottages so expensive I'd seen them listed in the real estate section of the New York Times Magazine. From the boulevard we looked down on them literally. I had no doubt their wealthy owners looked down on us locals figuratively.

It took us about fifteen minutes to get to the park. I asked Mel to take us to the railroad bridge above the main falls. We passed the overlook where visitors can view the main falls as it drops two hundred and fifteen feet into a basin cut from rock walls nearly four hundred feet tall. Taller than Niagara Falls, it looks tame in the dry season, but a day or two after a hard rain or a major snow melt, water thunders over the ledge.

After passing the overlook we turned left at the 'T', crossing a stone bridge then parking in a little dirt lot next to it. A short walk on a path through the woods gets you to an abandoned railroad bridge that's just far enough back in the woods that it's hard to see from the road.

We walked out to the middle of the bridge. To the East, the dark-gray walls of the gorge tower two hundred feet above the river as it meanders toward the main falls and eventually Cayuga Lake, which I could see off in the distance. Looking west, I watched the river, swollen by recent rains, thunder over a waterfall beneath the railroad bridge.

For over a hundred years, the gorge had been associated with a world renowned symbol of romance. A train called the

Black Diamond, a favorite of honeymooners, made regular runs from New York City to Niagara Falls, stopping on this same railroad bridge so passengers could enjoy a view of the gorge while they ate lunch. Unfortunately no trace exists of the nearby Hotel that catered their lunches.

The scale and power of our surroundings made my problems seem trivial. They might have been forgotten altogether if Mel hadn't brought them out a few minutes later by asking me if Sara knew what her mother had done to Dean.

"No, and if it ever gets out, Mrs. Jennings would never forgive me."

"Isn't that going to make using it a little tricky?"

I caught her eye and nodded my head. She told me to put the shovel down.

"The Shovel?"

"What if something bad is lurking out there and you inadvertently dig it up and let it loose? How are you going to feel then?"

"Oh, Mel, I forgot to tell you. Rick's going with us tonight. He's meeting us at the Pine Tavern at seven."

I did not expect her reaction. "Good Lord, Andy, what were you thinking?"

"But, Mel, when you dropped me off this morning you said we were going back to the cabin tonight."

"You should've confirmed it, Andy. Now there isn't enough time left to get the shopping done."

"Shopping?"

"You don't really expect me to wear the same clothes I wore this morning?"

"But Mel, we'll be in the woods. It'll be dark. No one will see you."

"I'll see me in the mirror before we leave. And if I don't look good, I won't feel good. And you know what that means for you. Besides, we'll be in public."

"We will?"

"Last I knew, the Pine Tavern was a public place."

"Yeah, okay, Mel. But, do me a favor, don't clean the store out, or me either."

Half an hour later Mel dropped me at the office. I used the rest of the day to catch up on missed phone calls. When I got home at five, Mel was waiting to show me her new outfit. I feigned interest, but it's hard for me to get excited about stretch fabrics in solid black. The price tag for the top was showing.

Without thinking I said, "Isn't that top a little pricey for what we're doing tonight?"

She pooched her lower lip out. "You don't think I look good in this?"

"Mel, you'll be the talk of the woods for years to come."

Her scowl passed quickly, pushed aside by a new thought. "You'd better get ready, Andy, or we won't get there by seven."

I changed into a new black sweatshirt and matching black sweatpants then flopped down on the bed to wait for Mel, who was in the bathroom finishing her preparations.

The next thing I knew, she was standing over me shaking my leg, saying, "Wake up, Andy, it's time to go."

I blinked a few times and looked around. It was like looking through a grimy window.

She gave me a pat on the leg. "The stress is getting to you, isn't it?"

"It shows, does it?"

"You were snoring."

I didn't feel any sharper after going through the motions of getting up, so I asked Mel to drive. We headed north on Route 89 again. The Pine Tavern is a family-friendly place with views of Cayuga Lake. Located near Taughannock Park, it's been a favorite of the locals for years. Their burgers, made from beef that's freshly-ground on site daily and served on French bread with Thousand Island dressing, have been my favorite sandwich since I first had one.

It wasn't quite dark when we pulled into the parking lot just before seven o'clock. Clouds were blowing across the sky on a brisk north wind, probably out of Canada, so it would be a cold night. The moon was a giant orange-yellow disk near the horizon, it's glow shimmering on the choppy water of the lake.

I followed Mel in from the car. Her outfit was expensive but it did look good on her. I told her so.

"Ya think?" she asked, striking a pose."

"Yeah, but if you had a few more arms, you'd look like a spider."

"I am so flattered by that, Andy."

When I suggested she lure me into her web, she shook her head emphatically. "This outfit is much too expensive for that, Andy."

I followed her inside to a table with a view of the lake. When she was settled I reminded her that a cheaper outfit would have left us the option to play around.

"You would have me sacrifice looks just so we could mess around?"

"I don't know what I was thinking, Mel."

"Clearly, you weren't thinking clearly."

I told her she wouldn't have to wear it for long, that I'd even help her take it off. Her response was stony silence. She perused the menu. It was a sham; we'd been to the Pine Tavern too many times. Like the menus at Morey's and the Dragon's Nest, she knew his one by heart.

Ever since I'd gotten up from my nap I'd been feeling like someone had drugged me, so I ordered coffee, hoping some high-voltage caffeine would kick my brain out of neutral.

Rick came in a few minutes later. He sat next to Mel and gave us both a thorough once-over. "Damned if you two don't look like a couple of Ninjas."

The coffee wasn't exactly high octane, but it did get my brain firing on more than one cylinder. I told Mel and Rick that we needed to get a few things straight before we went to the cabin.

Mel's reaction, "Such as?" sounded more like a warning than a question.

"Such as, I'll be the one snooping around that place

tonight."

She pooched her lower lip out again. I raised my hand to block the objection I knew was coming, "I deal with evidence every day, Mel. I know what to look for and how to handle it."

She looked hurt, but it couldn't be helped.

I told Rick I wanted to take his Jeep, because, "The cabin is on a steep dirt road covered with loose gravel. Our car doesn't have the traction. And I think Mel should be the driver. That okay with you?"

Mel asked what Rick would be doing.

"He'll be my lookout."

Mel crossed her arms, said, "That's not fair. I'm the one who found the place."

After an uncomfortable silence Rick announced that he'd found out who owns the cabin. "Anyone want to hazard a guess?"

I shook my head. Mel glared at me.

"No? Well it's none other than Ginger's boss, Struthers, the guy who owns the Tender Loin."

Hearing the name Struthers was no surprise. I knew that he and Dean were connected some how. And it was confirmation that Rick had been right – that Ithaca's underworld was a small place. I wondered out loud where that piece of the puzzle fit.

Mel groaned. "Please, God, no more metaphors."

But the more I thought about it, the more I liked it. "Think about it, guys. It's as though we've been given pieces from two jigsaw puzzles and we're trying to assemble them without the pictures. We don't even know how many pieces there are. Hell, what it if it's all one puzzle?"

Mel rolled her eyes then let her head drop, in a cartoonish display of despair.

CHAPTER XVIII

I was enjoying the last bite of my burger when Mel pushed her empty coffee cup away and stacked up her dishes. "If we're going, let's go."

I did not share her enthusiasm. No doubt Mel had eaten fast because she was eager to get going. To me it sounded like trouble. While Rick and Mel headed for the car, I went to the bar to settle the tab and tip.

Rick opted to drive until we got near the cabin. Sitting up front in his Jeep, flashing more than a hint of a smile, Mel obviously considered this an adventure. Unusually animated, she checked her makeup, her hair, and the contents of her pocketbook. Rick, on the other hand, was approaching our outing with his usual quiet caution. I carved out a place to sit amid the junk in his back seat.

It would be at least a forty-five minute ride so I tried to relax, leaning back in the seat with my eyes closed, but the suspension in Rick's Jeep was so stiff my teeth snapped together every time we hit a bump, and Mel had turned the radio on loud so she could hear it over the road noise.

By the time we drove through Ithaca it was dark, the moonlight making rare short-lived appearances through the clouds. When we headed up Stone Quarry Road, twisting around to look out of the back window gave me a great panoramic view of Ithaca's and Cornell's lights as we climbed up South Hill.

An idea had been bouncing around in my head while I

bounced around in the back seat. "Mel, you don't by any chance have an aspirin bottle, do you?"

"Oh, poor Hon. Do you have a headache?"

"An idea, actually."

"Well that explains the headache. You shouldn't push yourself, Andy. You should leave the intellectual heavy lifting to me."

"It doesn't have to be a pill bottle. Any small container with good cap will do."

"I'm a woman. I carry a purse. In all likelihood, there's a container in there somewhere."

I gave her a few minutes before I complained about how long it was taking.

"You're more than welcome to do this."

"Neither of us want me getting lost in there."

"Why don't you tell me what you want it for while I root around for it?"

"The police collected traces of dirt from Sara's shoes. If I get a sample of the dirt from the driveway near the cabin and the lab can match it to the dirt on her shoes, it'll help to prove she was there."

"I like the way you think, Andy."

I told her not to get too excited, that it might be a common soil type. Mel pulled out a pill bottle, waved her hand in a grand gesture, and said, "Voilà. You can dump the pills out. They're probably past the expiration date anyway."

But when I reached for it, she pulled it away, asking me how I planned to get the soil sample.

"Use the bottle to scoop some up?"

"That's your whole plan?"

"Mel, I just need an ounce or two of dirt."

"But what if someone sees you bent over in the driveway scooping up dirt with a pill bottle. You don't think that'll look suspicious?"

"That's not what worries me about tonight, Mel."

By then we were less than a mile from the cabin. I told Rick to stop when we got to the top of the hill. "This is where you and I get out."

Mel asked what she was supposed to do.

"Drive to the bottom of the hill and find a place to park, preferably out of sight, and turn off the lights. If someone from the cabin drives by, they'll get suspicious if they see a car parked near their driveway. We'll radio when we're ready to be picked up."

"Why don't I just drop you off at the foot of the driveway?"

"If someone's home they might see the car lights stop, and I don't want them waiting for us."

At the crest of hill, Rick pulled the car to the side of the road and stopped. We took the gear out and tested the walkie-talkies and flashlights before Mel left. Rick and I walked over the crest of the hill, starting our descent into the valley, as the taillights of the Jeep disappeared on the winding road below. Moonlight occasionally broke through the thick cloud cover, disappearing and reappearing at odd intervals, creating bizarre patterns of animated shadows.

We entered the woods about fifteen feet above the driveway, close enough to follow it, but far enough away to be hidden by the woods. We stayed in the woods until we got to the garage. I stopped at the corner nearest the cabin to let Rick come up beside me then whispered to him to wait there.

Walking along the side of the garage, I stopped at a window to look in, but it was dark enough inside to make a mirror of the glass. I wondered what the fool in the reflection had been thinking when he'd agreed to do something so stupid.

Apparently one of Dean's cohorts was home. The truck I'd seen that morning was still parked in the driveway. I crossed the stretch of yard from the garage to the cabin to look in one of the windows on the back side of it, but once again, it was too dark inside and I saw the same fool looking back at me.

There was an evergreen bush the size of a small car in front of the next window. I managed to squeeze between it and the house. The room was dark, and I hoped, unoccupied. Holding my flashlight against the glass, I turned it on. Ropes dangling from the bedposts confirmed our suspicions about the place.

Light coming through a window in the back door suffused the area immediately outside it with a dim glow. With the pill bottle in one hand and the cap in the other, I walked cautiously toward the driveway. Bending down to get the sample I felt as exposed and vulnerable as the new guy in the prison shower. The driveway soil felt damp and spongy, like moist clay.

Relief flooded over me as I stood up to cap the bottle and leave, but the good feeling didn't last. In my haste to get back to the garage where I wouldn't be so exposed, I kicked something in the grass, making a noise loud enough to be heard in the next county.

I froze and looked back at the house. Someone pulled the curtains aside. Light spilled out of the window. I'd been seen for sure. Precious moments later I got myself moving, toward the woods. Floodlights came on. You'd have thought it was a prison break movie. I was lit up and still ten feet from the woods. It felt like running through waist-deep water. I crashed through the brush and into the woods at a dead run, making more noise than a bull moose.

Because getting lost in the woods could be deadly, I veered back toward the road. But out of shape and breathing hard, I stopped to catch my breath. Well hidden, or so I thought until I heard a gunshot nearby, loud as a cannon, reverberating through the woods. I heard a slug punch through leaves near me. The woods were an impenetrable black void, but I didn't dare turn on the flashlight. Groping my way like a blind man, I made scant progress.

I heard two men talking, behind me, but getting closer. I risked moving faster. The ground fell out from under me. I landed hard, splashing in shallow, rocky water, making too much noise. I got to my feet, stumbled across a small creek, scrambled up a muddy bank using branches to pull myself up. While I struggled on the embankment, a new sound filled the darkness; an engine being cranked.

It sputtered, was cranked again, sputtered again then roared to life. The noise faded. Then I heard someone moving through in the brush near me, looked back, saw a flashlight beam coming toward me. Things brushed against my legs. There would be bushes along the creek. I crawled into them, pulling my black wool cap down and turned my collar up. Then I waited, holding my breath to listen, expecting another gunshot. What would it feel like to be hit by a bullet? I didn't want an answer.

I heard brush crunched underfoot, maybe fifteen or twenty feet away. Then only the faint resonant sound of a truck somewhere in the distance. Otherwise the forest was deathly quiet. The flashlight beam was making wide sweeps of the area, and slowly, silently, getting closer.

A man's shoes appeared through the brush. I turned my head away. The flashlight beam skimmed over me then swung away then swung back. I waited an eternity. The footsteps moved away then paused then moved again, toward the creek.

But that didn't mean I was safe. I had to get to the road so Mel could pick me up. I headed down the hill at an angle, I hoped toward the road. But slowly, lest I fall again. Minutes went by. I had no idea how many. But Mel and Rick would be wondering what happened to me.

I did find the road. A minute or so later I spotted light moving through the woods about a hundred yards above me. Car lights swept around a curve, the sound too deep and resonant to be Rick's Jeep. I slipped back into the woods then turned away and waited. I risked a glance as it passed. It was the truck from the cabin. I stepped back into the road in time to watch red taillights disappear around the corner below me. I fumbled with the walkie-talkie trying to raise Mel or Rick, but to no avail. That was worrisome.

Not knowing how far down the hill Mel drove before she found a turnoff where the Jeep would be hidden, I headed uphill to find Rick. It would be a tough walk. My leg muscles already ached. The bruises didn't help. I hadn't even made it to the next curve when I heard the deep throaty sound of the truck coming back. I worked my way into the woods again. After checking the walkie-talkie to be sure it was off, I knelt down and faced away from the road. A flashlight beam shone past me into the brush, creating bizarre, frantic, patterns of light and shadow as it moved.

The truck passed. I waited for the sound to fade. I felt some relief when I stood up and stretched my legs and back. Walking up the hill was hard, harder than I had expected. My shoes slipped on the loose gravel strained my already aching legs. Despite the coolness of the night, my black pullover had become slimy from exertion. Cuts on my face from tree branches stung from the dripping sweat. I tried the walkie-talkie.

Mel answered. "Where the hell are you, Andy?"

"Somewhere below the cabin."

"On the road?"

"Yeah, but the truck just passed me going uphill toward the cabin. So watch for it."

I saw the Jeep's headlights first. Then I heard gravel hitting the undercarriage as it slid around the bend above me. It slid sideways toward me, not stopping until it was close enough to touch.

Mel stuck her head out of the window and grinned at me. "Need a lift, sailor?"

I got in the back and flopped down on the seat. "I need the Aspirin I dumped out of your bottle."

Rick asked Mel to trade with him so he could drive. Better him than me. I felt better with him driving in case we ran into the truck. He got us turned around and headed back to the Pine Tavern to get our car. For the next forty-five minutes I was punished by the Jeep's suspension.

I'd had a thought while riding back to the Pines. "Hey Rick."

"Yes, boss."

Mel told him that didn't sound right. I asked him to time the trip from Mrs. Jennings place to the cabin. On the way home Mel grilled me about what had happened. I told her I'd seen ropes on one of the beds, suggesting that Sara had been there, but nothing else. I did have a disturbing thought I kept to myself. I wondered if residue from the medicine in the pill bottle had contaminated the soil sample, rendering it useless. I planned to give it to Mike in the morning regardless. But I wasn't looking forward to that, because even though I could never have talked Mike into sending someone out there, he'd be angry at me for going. It was late by the time we got into bed. On the upside, it didn't leave enough time for anything else to go wrong.

CHAPTER XIX

Apparently Mel thought I should get up early again Thursday morning because I woke to her shaking me. "How long did you plan on sleeping?"

I had serious doubts about using my legs for anything as important as walking. I told her I needed a hot shower.

"I thought you smelled a little ripe."

When I came out of the bathroom, Mel was sitting on the bed. She had some fun at my expense. "You're walking like you got kicked between the goalposts."

She giggled as I struggled to get my pants on. When putting my socks on became agony, I asked her for help.

She did help, but said, "I can't believe I'm doing this," feigning disgust, at least I hoped it was affected.

"Face it, Mel. The day may come when I can no longer dress myself."

"That works both ways, Andy."

"Let's hope not, for your sake."

"What? You won't help me in my hour of need?"

"Think about it, Mel. I'll be able to take your clothes off whenever I want. And I'll be able to dress you any way I like. And there won't be a thing you can do about it."

That got an exaggerated frown from her. "Thanks, Andy, now I'm afraid of growing old."

I went to the window to look outside, walking as though I had casts on both legs. A gusty wind was blowing rain against the window. Water running down the glass made everything outside look wrinkled. Fog had settled in with the rain, dropping visibility to a few feet from the house. I bent over a chair to stretch out my leg muscles.

Mel offered to make us some breakfast while I finish dressing then suggested we go see Mike after we ate. An hour later, Mel and I were in Mike's office. I set the pill bottle on Mike's desk while Mel settled into his guest chair. I got a chair from the hallway. Mike picked up the bottle and turned it over in his hands while I told him about our outing, and the cabin, and that I'd gotten a tipoff about it from Reed. I left out the part about being shot at.

When I'd finished, Mike said, "You guys do know how to have a good time," but he was frowning.

I asked him to have his lab guys check the soil to see if it matched the soil on Sara's shoes.

Little age lines appeared next to his eyes and around his mouth. "Why bother? You were trespassing. It's inadmissible as evidence. You should know that, Andy."

"Would you have gone out there with your lab rats just because we suspected that's where Dean took Sara?"

He made a face then told us to wait there for him while he took it to the lab. When he came back, he said, "What possessed you to do something so stupid? Oh wait, that's right. You're the guy who went to meet Reed at a deserted warehouse after dark."

"We took Rick with us."

"Oh, and that makes everything okay, does it?"

Mike took a bottle of Aspirin out of his desk, tapped four or five of them into his hand then popped them in his mouth. I told him he shouldn't take aspirin without water, that it was bad for his throat.

He smiled. "It's interesting, what you choose to worry about."

Then he leaned back in his chair, the angle of the harsh ceiling light darkening the lines in his face, aging him ten years. His gray hair looked like spider webbing turned white by a hard frost and his breathing sounded heavier than usual.

I asked him if he would send someone out to the cabin.

"I haven't decided."

"Those two are probably accomplices of Dean's. Unless they're stupid, they'll clear the place of evidence."

"They saw you. That would make losing the evidence your fault, wouldn't it, Andy?"

I reminded him about the ropes on the bed posts

"Unless the law's changed, it's still legal to have wild sex with your girlfriend."

I asked him again to send someone out to the cabin.

"So they can lodge a formal complaint against you for trespassing?"

I stood up to leave.

"Sit down, Andy, we're not quite done."

I sat.

Mike's face turned a worrisome shade of red. "Francis called me this morning. He was mad as hell, worse even than his usual theatrics. It seems he had planned to talk with Jennings about something, but you got to her first, got her set against him."

"I warned Mrs. Jennings that he would probably make Sara testify against Dean. I'm sorry you got caught in the crossfire, Mike, but Francis doesn't normally check with me before he does something stupid."

"I'll let that slide, but stay away from Jennings and the cabin."

Mel and I left then. Even though the rain had stopped, everything was still wet and the sun was out, making the landscape look vibrant. On the way back down the hill toward Ithaca, our wipers beat a steady rhythm as they cleared spray from the cars in front of us. Behind us, we trailed our own giant vortex of road spray.

I dropped Mel off at our house. Back at the office I took a good look at my empty waiting room. I had always thought that expensive decorations in a waiting room sent the wrong message about fees, but my waiting room looked dated and a little shabby, and that wasn't the image I wanted either.

Anne had a book open on her desk. She uttered a little "oh" when I walked in, as though I'd startled her. She did not look happy. "I thought maybe you'd left town," she said. "I've rescheduled so many appointments I'm rescheduling the rescheduled ones."

She pushed the appointment book across the desk toward me. "I need a new book. I've crossed out so many entries I can't read this one any more. Maybe you should get me an Etch-A-Sketch. I could just hold it up and shake it when it's full of scratched out appointments."

She was exaggerating. Not that I doubted her frustration. I just don't get that many appointments. I promised to make it up to her, and although I had no idea when or how, I meant it.

A picture of her daughter displayed prominently on the front of her desk reminded me just how lax I'd been as her boss; I couldn't remember the last time I'd asked her about her personal life. That was something I could fix. I sat in one of my own guest chairs and asked Anne about her daughter. "She's in college somewhere out west, right?"

She drifted off into an accounting of her daughter's classes and her archaeology internship, but soon ran out of steam, sitting silently, staring at her daughter's picture. When I stood up to make my exit, she said, "Hold on, Andy," as she shuffled through a pile of notes, holding one out to me. "Francis called. He wants you to call him back. He sounded mad, even more so than usual."

Recalling my talk with Mike, I suspected Francis just wanted the pleasure of chewing me out himself. I asked her if there was anything else.

"Maybe you could do something about these." Anne picked up a handful of notes and dropped them on the desk. They floated down like autumn leaves. I asked her to be patient a little longer then left.

I called Francis first, to get it over with. His secretary

put me right through, so I knew he wanted blood. I feigned ignorance, even tried to sound cheerful. "What can I do for you, Francis?"

"What the hell is wrong with you, Andrew?"

"I'm fine, Francis, thanks for asking."

"Jennings called me yesterday and gave me a ream of shit about her daughter testifying."

"Can you blame her?"

"You stay away from them, Andrew."

"You'll put Sara on the stand to tell her story so the press presents you as Ithaca's guardian of defenseless children."

Francis got the last word in before the line went dead. "So help me, Andrew, if you interfere with this case, I will have you arrested."

Threatening to have me arrested was classic Francis. There was no law against me talking to Jennings, and even if there was, it wouldn't stop me.

I spent a few minutes admiring the hydrangea bushes outside my office window in my neighbor's back yard. They were covered with huge white blossoms every summer because he had the time and the patience to deadhead them. Now the tiny petals on the dinner-plate size blossoms had turned pink with the changing of the season.

I returned some of the phone calls Anne had given me notes for, so they wouldn't call and bother her again. Then at eleven o'clock I called Mrs. Jennings.

She said she didn't want any more bad news.

"Mrs. Jennings, I think you should get Sara a lawyer if she doesn't already have one."

Her voice sounded clipped and anxious. "Why would she need a lawyer, Mr. Lee?"

"She should have someone watching out for her, Mrs. Jennings, someone who doesn't have an agenda. I have a friend who works with a victim's rights group. She's got experience with this sort of thing, and most important of all, she's tough. Francis won't be able to push her around."

"I can't afford a lawyer, Mr. Lee."

"She'll work with you on that. Please, don't decide anything until you hear what she has to say."

I gave her the woman's name and number and said goodbye. I felt a little better about Sara after that.

CHAPTER XX

Knowing that the blue pickup truck was somehow tied to the Tender Loin, I drove by the club on the off chance the truck was there. When I didn't see it parked on the street out front, I drove around the block to check the rear parking lot. Sure enough, it was there. I wrote down the license plate number then drove back around the block to park on the street in front of the club.

The word 'club' suggests a certain level of sophistication, but from the outside, the Tender Loin looked like an X-rated bookstore that had gone belly up. The only business sign was a piece of cardboard hanging on a loop of string inside the front door window, with the name written free-hand in magic marker. The picture windows were covered with brown shipping paper. The place next door to it really was boarded up. The whole neighborhood was run down, good material for a poster depicting urban decay.

I was backlit by sunlight when I stepped inside the club, which was as dark as a cave. Daylight spilling into the room around me created a small bright spot at my feet, in an otherwise gloomy interior. The air inside felt oppressive. Not the same oppressive you get when the sun comes out after a summer downpour. This oppressive was made of cigar smoke, stale beer and sweat.

The bartender, a heavyset woman of indeterminate age with a ruddy complexion, stood behind the bar near the door. She hadn't taken advantage of the customary gender enhancers, like makeup or jewelry, to soften her masculine appearance, and her hair was hidden under a baseball cap. For a female bartender in this place, the masculine look had to be a plus.

A mirror behind the bar ran the full length of it, affording anyone sitting at the bar a view of the stage, which was situated along the wall of papered-over picture windows. I sat on a stool midway down the bar; the only person at the bar except for a big man and a small woman who were standing at the far end of it, and too far apart to be a couple.

When the bartender came over I ordered a Coke. After hesitating for a moment, during which she looked at me as though she might take a slug at me for ordering such a cheap drink, she used a drinking glass to scoop ice cubes out of a bin underneath the bar then filled it with a dark liquid from a spray hose.

Slamming the drink down on the bar in front of me so hard some of the dark liquid splashed on the bar, she said, "Four dollars," testily, challenging me to complain about the price.

Even allowing for a cover charge, the price was a little steep, especially for such a dive. She scooped up my twenty with the speed and precision of a striking snake, taking it to the register to put in the cash drawer, or, more likely, her pocket, since she had blocked my view of the cash register. She did go through the motions. I heard the cash drawer ding when she closed it, which only proved that the bell worked.

On her way back to her perch near the front door, she put a stack of beer-soaked dollar bills in front of me. I hadn't planned to leave a sixteen dollar tip, but I didn't want my wallet to smell like old beer.

She put one foot up on the rung of a stool then leaned on the bar and looked out the front door window, as though she was watching the non-existent traffic outside. I suspected that she'd ventured to that nether land one step above unconsciousness where disappointments are forgotten and images projected on her retinas blurred before reaching her brain.

I walked over to her, leaving the Coke and soggy cash on

the bar. I figured she'd keep track of it for me because some portion of it would be her tip.

When I asked her where I could find Struthers, I saw a subtle change in her expression, but it didn't give away any information, and neither did she. "He's not here."

I asked her when she expected him.

"I don't. But you can leave a message."

Unable to think of a meaningful message, I went back to my stool to think about my next move. She went to talk to the young woman at the other end of the bar, the two of them looking at me several times during their short conversation. I sat on the bar stool with my back to the floor show, making circular motions with my glass, watching the questionable black liquid swirl while I waited to see what they had planned.

In the mirror behind the bar, I saw a young woman come out of the darkness at the other end of the room. She mounted the unfinished, plywood platform that passed for a stage. Billed as 'exotic' on a poster tacked to the utility pole out front, she looked about as mysterious as white bread.

Eyes closed, swaying dreamily to a song from the prior decade, she was probably in a drug-induced stupor. Since it was the start of her act, she hadn't shed any clothes yet, and since she hadn't, most of the patrons ignored her.

A group of collegiate-looking young men sat around a table near the stage. When their conversation subsided, they glanced at the dancer, but most of the time, they seemed more interested in their table talk. Two people sat in the darkness at the back of the room, silhouettes leaning in so close they might have been a couple, except that this wasn't the kind of place to bring a date. Most likely she was for hire. They showed no interest in the dancer, unlike the young man wearing workingman's clothes who sat off by himself nursing a beer. He watched the dancer with disturbing intensity.

Out of the corner of my eye, I noticed the woman who'd been talking to the bartender walking toward me wearing high heels and a long black robe with bright red dragons on it. The empty glass in her hand had a cheap plastic umbrella in it. I doubt she'd ever been to a place where the umbrellas they put in your drink are made of wood. Of Asian descent, she was so small and fine-boned, that as long as you didn't look too closely, she could probably pass for an underage girl, which no doubt was an asset with some of the patrons.

She put the empty glass down on the bar next to me. I knew the dance. I held the glass up to signal the bartender for a refill. The bartender, who'd been watching for the signal, promptly took the glass away and refilled the glass with whatever had been in it earlier. It would not be cheap.

The Asian woman told me her name was Kitty. That was unlikely, but there wasn't anything to be gained by calling her on it. I asked her who owned the blue pickup truck parked out back. She shrugged her shoulders.

When I told her I'd pay for the information, she took a close look at my face. "I know all the cops around here."

I told her I was a lawyer and that I represented Ronnie Dean.

In an instant the look on her face changed from mild curiosity to alarm. She told me to talk to the big man at the end of the bar. The bartender put Kitty's refill in front of us, taking most of my soggy bills away with her. Kitty walked away with her new drink.

The guy at the end of the bar was taller up close, and muscular looking, with a dozen or more tattoos on his neck and arms. He gave me a quick sideways glance when I leaned on the bar next to him. The dark stubble on his chin was on the verge of becoming a beard. I asked him if he owned the blue pickup parked in the alley out back.

Two small black orbs under a thick brow ridge looking out at me over a nose that had been broken at least once, eyed me with suspicion. "Who wants to know? he asked."

I told him I was Dean's lawyer and held out my hand. I harbored no illusions that he would shake it, which he didn't. That was okay with me. His expression changed subtly as he stood up. He seemed suspicious of my intent but not sure what to do about it. After warning me that I was "messing with the wrong people," he left the room.

I walked past my bar stool and would have left if a man hadn't appeared out of the dark then, from the same place the dancer had. Shorter and heavier than the man I'd just been talking with, he had a head full of unruly hair and looked as though he'd gotten dressed in a panic, or possibly dressed by a child. His shirt was twisted at the waist because his shirttails had been tucked in crooked, and he had missed a belt loop then pulled his belt too tight, bunching his pants up on one side.

He leaned on the bar. I walked over and stood next to him, watching him in the mirror behind the bar to avoid making direct eye contact. I asked him who owned the blue truck in the lot out back.

While nearly every part of his body fidgeted, he said, "Sometimes Jack lets me ride in it," with the eagerness of a boy bragging about his father.

Although the contrast between his deep voice and his child-like enthusiasm was disconcerting, and his response had been obtuse, I had learned the owner's first name. I asked him if Jack was around.

"Just left."

I figured he meant the big guy who had warned me off. I told him my name was Andy and asked him what his name was.

"My name's Nate. Ain't it great?"

"And what about Mr. Struthers, Nate, is he here?"

"Sometimes Bobby has a job for us. Then I go with Jack in his truck. Jack's mean to me sometimes, but I go with him anyway. I do it for Bobby. He's my brother."

I was about to ask him where I could find Struthers when the bartender interrupted us, saying "Nate" then nodding her head toward the door at the far end of the room where he had come from. He skulked away like a disappointed child.

The bartender looked at me askance. "Mister, you need to leave."

I left the rest of my soggy cash on the bar. It felt good to be outside in the fresh air. A few minutes later I was back at my office.

I had no sooner spread papers from the Eams case on my desk then Anne knocked and leaned into my office. "Rick called earlier." She handed me a slip of paper. "You can reach him at this number."

I thanked her and made the call.

Risk answered on the second ring. "Andy, you'll never guess who called me last night."

"What do I win if I get it right?"

"Ginger's here at the No-Tell Motel. You need to hear what she has to say."

Anne poked her head in again. "Your wife's on the other line."

I held my hand over the mouthpiece and whispered to her. "Ask her to hold for a minute."

Then I rejoined the conversation with Rick. "You mean the sleazy motel on Route 13 South with a swimming pool that looks like a frog pond?"

"Room four."

I told him to stay put; that I'd be there as soon as I could then punched the button for the other line. "Feel like taking a ride, Hon?"

I went out through the waiting room past Anne's desk so she'd know I'd left.

She seemed surprised. "Leaving so soon, Andy?"

I told her I wasn't sure when I'd be back then went outside to wait for Mel. When Mel picked me up I told her to head south on Route 13. She asked where we were going. Rather than raise her stress level ahead of time, I told her about going to the Tender Loin, and about Jack and Nate. She told me she'd checked with the rest of the people on the security listing but hadn't had any luck.

"So that whole security card business was legit after all."

"Sorry, Andy, but your client's guilty."

About the time we passed the entrance to Buttermilk Park on our left, Mel said, "I've got some more news, but you're not going to like it."

"Such as?"

"Such as your friend Arthur called our house today."

"I thought I asked you not to refer to him as my friend?"

"He called today; wanted to chat."

"Sorry Mel, that's my fault. He's been calling me at work and I haven't returned his calls. But why should that upset me?"

"When he told me his name, I assumed he wanted to speak with you, so I told him you weren't there."

"And?"

"And he invited me over to his place to show me his collection of auto parts calendars."

Mel told me to watch my blood pressure, but it was too late. Unfortunately, that's when the No-Tell Motel appeared ahead on our right. It was the kind of place where you rented rooms by the hour, where they didn't expect you to use your real name, and if you called the place, it didn't matter who you asked for, he wasn't registered there.

I pointed at it and told her to pull in next to room four. Mel asked me what we were doing there of all places, and from the tone of her voice it was clear that I was already in trouble. Aside from it being the sleaziest place Mel had ever set foot in, Ginger was in there. Mel pulled up in front of room four, next to the only other car in the parking lot.

She shut off the car and turned sideways in her seat to face me. "That Rick's Jeep, isn't it?"

I said, "Yeah," then got out of the car quickly and walked to the door, hoping to avoid any more questions.

Soon after I knocked, I saw Rick pull the curtains back. Mel got there just as he opened the door to a room even more squalid than what I'd imagined. I held the door open to let Mel go in ahead of me. When I closed it behind us, a bolt latch that was hanging by one loose screw tapped against the jamb.

There was just one bed in the room. The bedspread piled

up at the foot of it revealed sheets as soiled as the mud flaps on a farm truck. An overstuffed chair by the door that had lost a significant portion of its of stuffing, had probably started out a shade of beige then turned the telltale dingy-yellow of material that has spent years in the presence of heavy smokers. The coffee table next to it had a broken leg propped up under it at a slant and held in place with duct tape.

The single bare bulb in the ceiling fixture gave off a murky glow like candlelight. The plastic curtains on the windows were torn and dingy, and there was a hole in the bathroom door where the door knob should have been.

But the worst part was the smell. It hit me like a hammer, even after the appearance had lowered my expectations to the level of manure. Thankfully I couldn't place it. And then there was the knowledge that all of the beds in the establishment were only used for the exchange of bodily fluids. That would bother Mel more than all the rest of it.

A look of disbelief settled on Mel's face as she surveyed the room. She started to say something but Ginger came out of the bathroom then. Mel mouthed a few inaudible words as Ginger sat on the bed.

Ginger's slacks and tank top had the appearance of a designer outfit. Reddish-orange hair the color of hot embers, framed her face. I avoided letting my eyes linger on her because Mel already looked hot enough to ignite.

I told Ginger she'd better have a good explanation for coming back.

"I was doing my act at a club in Rochester last night. Of course it was dark in there, but I noticed a guy sitting in the back of the room because the light shone on him when someone opened the door. I'd seen him talking to Struthers before, so when I got done with my act, I slipped out the back door. I didn't even go back for my stuff. I hitchhiked back here and called Rick."

The guy must have been calling other strip clubs in the area looking for her. In the meantime, I knew Mel had just added a new entry to the balance sheet covering our relationship, and I'd find it in the column labeled, "You Owe Me Big Time." I asked Ginger what she wanted.

Her response sounded like a confused mix of anger and desperation. "Maybe I didn't tell you everything last time, but what I did tell you was true."

Mel's hands were squeezing her purse straps so hard her knuckles had turned white. "What do you mean; maybe you didn't tell us everything? Don't you know?"

I hadn't seen Mel that mad in years. Ginger, on the other hand, seemed remarkably composed for someone without any prospects, but she had no doubt been living on the edge of financial and psychological ruin for years. Ginger told us that something strange had happened at the club the night Arthur's wife was killed. "Struthers came to see me that night before I danced. He told me Arthur would be coming to my room after I danced, and that I should keep him there all night. He made it real clear that something bad would happen to me if I didn't. You can't imagine the things I did to keep him from leaving"

If she was telling truth, Arthur couldn't have killed his wife. She paused there with her eyes locked on mine, as though she wanted or expected some sort of approval. I told her that, if she had another card to play, she'd better play it because she wouldn't get another chance. She looked timid and scared. It was probably just an act, but it was a convincing one.

What she told us next was definitely intriguing. "Struthers told me to put Arthur's keys under a towel in the bathroom down the hall. Taking his keys was easy because Arthur never puts his pants on to go to the john. And I told Arthur I wasn't feeling well so I could make extra trips to the john without him getting suspicious. The keys were gone when I went back at around midnight. I found them back under the towel sometime between two and three, and put them back in his pocket the next time he went to the john. He never suspected a thing."

If true, it explained how Arthur's car was spotted at the

boyfriend's place. Knowing that she'd be naming the killer, I asked her who had taken the keys from the bathroom.

She shrugged her shoulders. "How would I know? I was with Arthur, remember?"

"Would one of the other girls at the club know?"

"Not likely."

I told Rick to talk with the girls at the club on the chance one of them had seen or heard something. Then I gave Ginger a warning. "If the person who took those keys killed Arthur's wife, you're an accomplice to murder."

"Yeah, I could go to prison. I get that. I'm not stupid. But, think about my situation, Mr. Lee. There's only one way Struthers can be sure I won't talk."

She was right. She had reason to worry. And yet, she studied her fingernails as though she was overcome with boredom. I took the opportunity to ask her about Jack.

"The guy's a perv."

I asked for something more specific.

"Him and Nate do Struthers' dirty work."

When I asked her what she meant by dirty work she shot me a look of exasperation. "God, don't you ever stop with the questions?"

I lied to her, told her we were almost done.

After some theatrics, including a half-audible profanity, she told us, "Struthers put video cameras in the rooms where we take our customers. He told us he did it for our protection, but one of the girls caught him watching."

"Anything else you can tell us about him, Ginger?"

"He's too rough."

"As in physically abusive?"

"Well, yeah, what else would I mean?"

I asked her why Struthers would get mixed up in the murder of Eams' wife.

She shrugged her shoulders, said, "No idea" then stood up, adjusting the fit of her slacks and tank top. She asked how much longer we'd be. I asked her if there was anything between Eams

145

and Struthers.

"Eams never pays for sex with me or for his drinks. That's all I know."

I got the feeling Ginger didn't have much more in the way of valuable information and gave up digging. Since Mel and I got there Rick had been standing quietly off to the side. I gave him three large bills and told him, "Don't feel as though you need to spend it all, but find someplace fit for humans where she'll be safe. I've seen landfills nicer than this."

Ginger thanked me, but grudgingly. To placate Mel, I told her I'd bill Eams for it.

I headed for the door, had just reached for the doorknob when Ginger told me, "Don't think for a second you can get me to testify."

"If you did, we'd put them in prison. They'd never bother you again."

"I doubt that," she said, "and why should I risk getting killed to help Arthur? He's no better than the rest of them."

I couldn't stand being in that foul-smelling room any longer, so I wished Ginger luck and held the door open for Mel. On the way to the car I told her, "Let's pay Arthur another visit."

Outside, the weather had deteriorated into a steady light drizzle, leaving the landscape looking blurred and gray. But after the stench of the motel room, even wet earth and rotting leaves smelled good.

"Andy," Mel said, as she got behind the wheel, "I can't find the words to describe that place."

"Yeah, it's bad."

"Toxic waste site bad."

"Sorry, Mel."

"Andy, if you touched anything in there it's the end of our sex life."

She got us out of the parking lot and headed north on Route 13.

I asked her what she thought of Ginger this time.

"She was probably telling the truth."

146

Mel would never agree, but learning that someone had lifted Arthur's keys the night Sheila was killed, made up for the discomfort of the motel room. Now I wanted to ask Arthur if there was a connection between him and Struthers.

CHAPTER XXI

As Mel pulled into the parking lot outside Arthur's office she said, "I'll bet you're the first guy ever, to pay for Ginger's room and not get laid."

"Is that why you were so quiet on the way over here? You were working on the punch line?"

"Admit it, Andy; she's got a nice body"

I could lie, tell her Ginger wasn't much to look at, but that would never fly, or I could tell her Ginger looked great, which was the truth, but it was also a bad idea.

I took the coward's way out. "I've seen a lot of good-looking women over the years, Hon, but not one of them turned my head like you do."

She smiled; a faint smile, but a smile is a smile. I gave her a peck on the cheek before getting out of the car.

The receptionist wasn't at her desk when we entered. I wondered if she was in Arthur's office. His door was ajar. Just before we got to it I heard Arthur say, "You'll be working some overtime tonight."

He sounded out of breath, a clue that going in without knocking was a bad idea, but the thought registered a moment too late. I regretted it. Arthur's receptionist was standing next to his desk and Arthur's hand was out of sight, someplace it shouldn't have been.

I was embarrassed. Mel was apoplectic. Unlike his sleazy, oversexed receptionist, who blushed as she hurried out past us,

Arthur did not appear to be embarrassed; proud maybe, but definitely not embarrassed. He stood up and came around the desk holding out the same hand that had been somewhere up his secretary's skirt. Knowing Mel would never allow me to touch her if I touched that hand, I ignored it.

I expected Arthur to take it as an insult. He didn't, behaving instead as though we were long lost friends. "Andy, I was getting worried about you. I must've called your office twenty times."

I tried to keep my voice even and noncommittal. "Mel told me you called our house."

"What was I supposed to do? You didn't answer any of the messages I left you."

"You invited her to your house to look at your posters."

"Like I told the little lady, we're all friends here."

"No, Arthur, we're not, and the next time you pull a stunt like that, you'll be looking for a new lawyer."

"Hey," he said, holding his hands up with his palms out toward me. "I'm one of the good guys, remember?"

"I seriously doubt that, Arthur."

"I'm sorry you feel that way, Mr. Lee."

I got to the reason for our visit. "It looks as though you were framed."

"Hell, that's what I've been trying to tell you."

"Well don't get too excited. The DA isn't going to drop the murder charge just on my say so."

As he took out a checkbook, he said, "Tell me how much you need."

"All I need today, Arthur, is information."

"Such as?"

"Such as, what's your connection to Struthers?"

Arthur began fidgeting like an eight-year-old boy forced to sit through a long church sermon. "What's that got to do with Sheila's murder?"

"Humor me, Arthur."

"You're wasting time, Mr. Lee; time that would be better

149

spent figuring out who killed my wife."

"What I've got isn't enough to keep you out of prison, and let's face it, Arthur, a guy like you would have a bad time in prison."

Arthur frowned, as though he was working through a difficult problem. Then he tipped his head a little to one side and squinted at me. "You've been talking to one of the girls at the club, haven't you? That's why you asked me about Struthers."

I realized then that asking him about his connection to Struthers may have put one or more of the dancers in danger, but it was too late to put the cat back in the bag. I repeated the question.

He looked at me for a long moment then his expression suddenly reverted to his usual pokerfaced indifference and he asked me if I thought Struthers had something to do with Sheila's murder.

"I think it's a possibility."

"Andy, you can't believe half of what those girls tell you. Hell, for a few bucks, they'll do or say anything you want. It's as natural to them as collecting honey is to a bee."

"That's why relying on Ginger for your alibi should frighten you."

Arthur stood up as if our meeting had ended. "We're running out of time, Mr. Lee, and you're chasing ghosts."

I stood up to leave, but waited for Mel to lead to the way so I'd be between her and Arthur. While I waited for her, I told him, "Bees collect nectar, Arthur, not honey."

He looked at me as though I had six heads and twelve arms.

Outside, I saw rain off to the east, but the sky had cleared in the west and the sun was shining. Someone somewhere was looking at a rainbow. A few tiny wisps of steam rose off the pavement. If it had been a hot day, steam would have been rising in clouds, and it would have been unbearably muggy. Luckily for us, the incoming Canadian air was cool and dry.

Back in the car, as Mel dug through her purse for the keys,

she asked me if we had accomplished anything.

"Only if you count putting the girls at the club in danger."

"You think so?"

"I'll bet Arthur's sitting in there right now wondering which one of them talked to us."

"Andy, aren't you always saying that we shouldn't take responsibility for situations that aren't our doing? Well, I think you should take your own advice."

"Hey, no fair using my own lines against me."

"It's not your job to undo everything that's gone wrong in those girl's lives."

Her comment had been out of character. "Are you okay, Mel?"

"I just wish we could get on with our own lives, Andy."

We went to the office next, but by then it was too late in the day to start anything new, so I told Mel I'd meet her upstairs in the apartment in a few minutes. I wanted to check with Anne before she left for the day.

Anne told me Francis had called again, that he wanted me to call him back ASAP. We all have our share of unpleasant things to do. Talking to him was one of mine.

Even though he kept me waiting on the phone, I tried my best to sound pleasant, at least until I knew what he wanted. "To what do I owe the pleasure this time, Francis?"

"I hope you enjoy being on the losing end."

"Why? What did I lose?"

"Your case, hot shot."

"You want to tell me what happened, Francis?"

"I got Dean to sign a confession."

I wondered what in the name of all that was holy Dean had been thinking. "And what did he confess to?"

"That he raped Sara Jennings."

I wouldn't have been more speechless if I'd been kicked in the groin.

"Hey, Andrew, you still there?"

I didn't give him the courtesy of a response, because

151

anything I said would give him an opening to insult me again. But, good old Francis, he was just too full of himself to let it go. "You have to know how to play these clowns."

I asked him what he gave Dean in return.

"Not a thing. Like I've told you before, you should leave it to the professionals."

It didn't make any sense. Dean had acted both surprised and angry when he heard Sara had been molested. Why would he confess to it if he didn't do it? Of all people, Dean would know how judges and juries feel about people who commit crimes against children.

While I struggled with the contradiction, Francis took the opportunity to rub salt in my wound. "The hearing is set for Tuesday morning. But you might as well sleep in because Dean doesn't want you there. Just think, Andrew, you got fired by a guy who's such a waste, the doctor probably apologized to his mother when he was born. How does that make you feel?"

I imagined Francis having a few extra drinks at his private club after work, imagined him droning on at length about this latest victory to anyone drunk enough, or bored enough, to listen. I wasn't going to take it lying down. "If I were you Francis, I'd keep this low key, because I think you're the one being played here."

"Do not talk to Dean, or Sara, or her mother. Is that understood, Andrew?"

Although I'd had enough of his smug attitude, I still took the high road by saying, "It looks like you won this round, Francis." Then I hung up on him.

Mel would be glad I was free of Dean, but I felt slighted by Dean's confession, not to mention bewildered. I took the back stairs up to the apartment where I found Mel sitting on the couch in the living room. I sat down next to her. I didn't pretend things were okay. I knew she'd see right through it if I did.

"What's wrong, Andy?"

I told her about Dean's confession.

That got a startled, "Oh," followed by a pause then, "So,

what happens now?"

All I could do was shrug my shoulders.

"Aren't you glad to be rid of him, Andy? I know I am."

"Francis has proved once again that you don't have to be stupid to do stupid things."

"Meaning what, exactly?"

"Well one thing is certain, Mel, Dean wouldn't have signed that confession unless there was an advantage in it for him. But Francis is so full of himself he can't see that."

"Gee thanks, Andy, that really cleared things up for me."

Mel's calm, reassuring presence was just what I needed to drive out the anger and disappointment I felt after my talk with Francis. But knowing that I couldn't correct the imbalance in the scales of cosmic justice that Dean's actions had caused would bother me no end. "We still don't know what happened that night. Mel."

"Who cares what happened?"

"I'd like to know why Dean confessed now."

"Again, I say, who cares?"

"Dean must have known someone was getting too close."

"Too close to what?"

"Too close to the truth, Mel. That's why he cut the deal with Francis."

"Am I going to like where this is going?"

"You should."

"And why is that, Andy?"

"We've been turning over a lot of rocks."

Mel patted my leg and smiled. "Why don't you lie down and put your head on my lap, and try to avoid any more metaphors."

"Oh, and just so you know. According to Francis, Dean fired me."

"What, you're not good enough for that scumbag?"

"I'll say it again, Mel. Why would Dean confess?

"The way I see it," Andy, "a bad guy did some bad things and now he's going to jail. Case closed."

153

"How can we be sure these guys pay for their sins if we don't have an accounting of their sins?"

"Andy, please, unless you know the outcome would be significantly improved by digging up the past, let it go."

"You know I can't do that, Mel."

"That doesn't leave much time to solve the case."

"When you read a mystery novel, you can tell how close you are to the solution by the number of pages left in the book. Unfortunately, we don't know how many pages are left in this book."

"You felt the need to punish me with another metaphor?"

"I can't help it if I'm erudite."

"Really, Andy? Scholarly?"

A few moments later, she said, "That Francis is a real shit, isn't he."

"Oh, don't worry about Francis, Hon. He'll play this out in a bunch of news bytes choreographed to appear spontaneous, and scripted to make him look tough on crime. But I'll guarantee you Dean got something he wanted from Francis, and Francis is going to look foolish when that comes out."

Mel leaned over into me, kissing my neck then put her head on my shoulder. I held her quietly and stroked her hair, and thought about how good it would feel to give in to the passion.

After a while she sat up and turned to face me. "I think we should have dinner delivered and spend a quiet evening here."

It was a tempting offer; not as exciting as wild steamy sex, but restorative. And who knew where it might lead? Unfortunately, I wouldn't be able to relax knowing Dean might get off lighter than he should. Reluctantly, I pulled free of her embrace and told her I needed to get back to the office.

"That's not fair," she said, with a pouty but playful look.

Imaging an hourglass with the sand nearly drained, I apologized profusely and left. On the way down to my office to see if Anne had left for the day, I counted the years since I'd started my practice. For fifteen years I'd been kidding myself about making the world a better place.

Anne asked me something when I entered the reception room, but I missed it because counting the years had led me to an epiphany, which I noted out loud. "The trial was sixteen years ago."

She tipped her lead a little and frowned. "Are you okay, Andy?"

"I couldn't believe I hadn't seen it sooner. To see if my hunch was right I'd have to confront Mrs. Jennings in spite of Francis' warning. I thanked Anne then hurried upstairs to find Mel.

Still nestled on the couch, Mel put her arms out. "I was hoping you'd come back."

Tomorrow would wait.

CHAPTER XXII

Next morning, Mel sat across from me at the kitchen table in a pink bathrobe drinking some extra-dark coffee. "You look happy, Andy, and if you're smart, you'll tell me it's because last night was the best sex you've ever had."

"It was."

"And?"

"And what, Mel."

"I know you, Andy. You're feeling smug about something."

"I wouldn't go that far."

"Are you going to share your good fortune with me, or not?"

"I figured out one piece of the puzzle. It had been right under my nose all along, but hard to see amid the chaos created by Dean."

"Did you figure out who killed Eams' wife?"

"No, Mel, but I think it's about connections."

"Why don't you let me in on it?"

I laid it out for her. When I'd finished, she asked me what I planned to do about it.

"What we've got is a lot of players with a stake in the outcome of the game. I think we need to bring them all together and turn up the heat, get them interacting, like the molecules in a boiling liquid."

She looked up at the ceiling and raised her arms in a gesture of supplication. "Please God, deliver me from the metaphors."

"What I really want to do, Mel, is get them all in the same place then watch the fireworks."

"Do you think mixing bad metaphors clarifies anything, or do you do it just to drive me nuts?"

I left her to finish her coffee and took mine downstairs to the office. It wasn't quite seven o'clock. I had about an hour before Anne would be in. At ten to eight, I heard Anne and went out to the waiting room to talk with her. When I got there she was hanging her coat in the closet and hadn't heard me come in.

When she turned around and saw me she gasped. "Jesus, Andy, you really scared me."

I was glad to see her, had been thinking that talking to her would probably be the high point of the day. The look on her face was a strange mixture of curiosity and concern, and like the day before, she asked me if I was feeling alright.

"I feel better than I have in days, but I need you to come to my office when you get settled. I have some things I want you to do for me."

She came in a few minutes later with her notepad and sat in a chair opposite my desk. Always the professional, she had on a dark, knee-length skirt and plain white blouse with her hair pinned up in a swirl.

"When you're ready, Mr. Lee" she said, her pen poised over her notebook.

I told her to call the temp agencies and book someone for the week of Thanksgiving. "Find someone who you think is pleasant enough and sharp enough to handle my calls and schedule my appointments. And when you've done that, call a travel agency and book a flight for you and your husband to Phoenix for that week."

She took in a quick breath. "Oh, Andy, we couldn't possibly afford that."

"We'll consider it your Christmas bonus."

"I don't know what to say."

"Have the temp start a day or two before you leave so you have time to train them." I put a credit card on the desk near her.

157

"Use my card to book your hotel room and rental car. And don't go cheap on the room."

"That's very generous, Andy."

"It's long overdue. Now, is there anything brewing here that I should know about?"

"There are a few new messages."

"Bring me the urgent ones. I'll dig into the rest of them on Monday. I hope to be back on my usual schedule next week."

After Anne left my office I stepped out the back door to see how the day was turning out. The morning sky was deep blue with only a few high white clouds. A cool, almost cold, breeze blowing in from the north carried the fresh clean scent of Canadian air.

Maybe it was time to take the big leap, plunge in the river and see where the current took me. For the young, the unknown seems fun and exciting, but for the rest of us its attraction diminishes rapidly with age, in a cosmic, inverse geometric progression.

I floundered for the rest of the morning and early afternoon trying to devise a plan that would force things to a satisfactory conclusion. Then sometime around 2:00 PM, Anne came to tell me that Arthur's secretary was on line two, and that she sounded frantic. The woman hadn't impressed me as the type to fluster easily, especially being a landlord's secretary.

I pushed the button for line two. "This is Andrew Lee."

"This is Patty, Mr. Lee, Arthur's secretary."

"What can I do for you, Patty?"

"Arthur just stormed out of here."

I was inclined to say, "Tell someone who cares," but said, "And?" instead, and left the word hanging.

"He keeps a gun in his desk. He was in such a state when he left I thought I should check for it. It wasn't there, Mr. Lee."

The image of her standing next to his desk popped into my head, an unwanted, uncomfortable distraction. "You should call the police, Patty."

"They won't do anything until after something bad

happens." She sounded desperate, on the verge of crying.

"What makes you think I can help?"

"He's mad because of something you said, Mr. Lee."

I asked her why she thought that.

"Because right after he talked to you yesterday, he left here angrier than I've ever seen him. When he came in this morning he still looked angry. I knew something was up because he only stayed for a couple of minutes. That's why I checked for the gun."

My mind raced through the conversation I'd had with Arthur the day before, searching for something I'd said that might have upset him. I asked her if she could remember anything else he said.

"When he walked past my desk he mumbled something about Struthers."

I remembered telling Arthur that I thought Struthers had been mixed up in his wife's death. It didn't make me responsible for whatever Arthur had in mind, but it did make me a victim of my own cause and effect logic. I told her again to call the police because the last thing I wanted to do was get between him and Struthers, especially if he had a gun.

Her voice sounded shaky when she told me that there would be a party at Struthers' place later that night. "I'm afraid he'll go there and do something stupid."

I didn't tell her what I was thinking; that it was damn decent of Arthur to provide the entertainment for Struthers' party. I told her I'd do what I could. She thanked me and hung up. I called Mike. He sounded curt and angry when he answered. It seemed that everyone was having a rough day. I told him his phone etiquette needed polishing.

"Make it quick, Andy."

"Arthur Eams' secretary just called. She said Arthur's got a gun. She thinks he plans to use it on Struthers."

"Gee, what a shame. Imagine how much easier my job would be if these guys killed each other off."

"Actually, Mike, you wouldn't have a job if they did that.

"Oh yeah, good point. Now what do you want, Andy?"

"There's a party at Struthers' place tonight. Arthur's secretary thinks he might show up there looking for Struthers."

Mike agreed to check on Arthur, see if he had a gun permit. "But that's about all I can do until he does something stupid."

"This is Eams we're talking about, Mike. The odds of him doing something stupid are pretty good."

"If you want something from me, tell me what it is. I don't have time for guessing games this morning."

"I'm going to crash Struthers' party. I hope you'll put in an appearance."

"And why would I do that?"

"Everybody who's mixed up in the Dean and Eams cases will be there, and it's all going to blow up in their faces."

"Yeah, what makes you think so?"

"Because I'm going to light the fuse. And if that isn't enough to get you out there, the thought of Eams and Struthers playing with guns should be."

"To tell you the truth, Andy, I'm not sure I care enough about them to give up my evening."

"Then do it so no innocent bystanders get hurt, like your good friends, Andy and Mel."

"What the hell have you got planned?"

I told him the party started at seven. "The fireworks should start soon after that."

My next call was to Mrs. Jennings. I told her I wanted to meet with her at seven o'clock to discuss the Dean case.

She said pretty much what I'd expected. "Why would I do that now?"

"Because your past doesn't want to stay buried."

"What the hell does that mean?"

"Mrs. Jennings, whatever Dean had planned, something went wrong. He wouldn't have confessed otherwise. It means that, once again, he'll be looking for revenge when he gets out of prison. That may be years from now, but if he found you and Sara once, he can do it again. Do you want that hanging over you?"

I listened to the muted sounds of birds chirping outside my window, and the ambient hum of the phone line.

"I'll help you confront your demons, Mrs. Jennings,"

"What is it you want from me, Mr. Lee?"

"Meet with me tonight."

She agreed, albeit reluctantly. I told her I'd pick her up at twenty minutes to seven. I called Anne's extension next to ask her if she had the number of the motel where Rick had put Ginger up. Ginger didn't answer until the sixth ring. I hoped the delay didn't in any way involve Rick.

"Ginger, this is Mr. Lee. I have a favor to ask."

Her voice sounded wary. "What is it you want, Mr. Lee?"

I told her that Struthers was having a party at seven o'clock, and that, "Everyone's going to be there."

"You want me to go to a party with you? You're asking me out on a date?"

"Good heavens no, Ginger. But I do want you there."

"Yeah? What's in it for me?"

"With your help, I can take all the bad guys off the playing board tonight."

"Including Struthers?"

"Including Struthers."

"What about Jack? Is he gonna be there?"

"I promise you you'll be safe, Ginger."

"Really, Mr. Lee. You're going to protect me from Struthers, and Jack, and Nate? Really?"

"A detective friend of mine will be there."

"What about the next day and the day after that. Who's going to protect me then?"

"If you do this tonight, we'll put them all someplace where they can't ever hurt you again. And if you're still worried after tonight, I'll give you a thousand dollars and a ticket to sunny California. How does that sound?"

I heard the hum of the phone line again. I was about to give up when she said, "Where?"

I told her we'd pick her up. Mel would be angry but I

needed Ginger there. Then she asked if Francis would be there. I couldn't imagine why she was worried about him, but told her not to be.

"If he's going," she said, "I'll go with him."

I assumed she meant it as a joke. I didn't get the humor. "With Francis? Are you kidding?"

"Francis has had his eye on me."

"You're serious?"

"You don't think I have the looks?"

I told her she had more than enough looks. What I couldn't understand was why she'd want to go anywhere with Francis. But I liked the idea of her showing up as his escort, especially in an election year, especially with wealthy campaign donors present.

"Tell you what," I said. "You call me if there's a problem getting Francis to take you. Otherwise, I'll see you there at seven, but whatever you do, don't tell Francis we talked."

I had one more call to make. Mel sounded impatient when she answered the phone.

"Mel, I want you to put on one of your classy but sassy outfits, some sweet-smelling fumes, and some sparkly baubles. You and I are going to crash a party."

She asked me where. Like Ginger, Mel sounded wary.

"Struthers' place."

"What makes you think I want to go there?"

"Well for one thing, Mel, everybody involved in the Eams and Dean cases will be there."

"That sounds like a good reason to stay home."

"I think I can wrap up both cases. I thought you'd want to be there for that."

"I'm kinda in the middle of something right now, Andy."

I told Mel we had to be there by seven and let her get back to whatever it was she was doing. Too distracted with thoughts about the party to focus on anything difficult, I went home early to make sure Mel would be ready on time.

CHAPTER XXIII

Mel must have heard me come in when I got home, because she came to meet me. I even got a hug. "Anne called," she said. "That was a nice thing you did for her."

"I probably got more mileage out of it than she did." I reminded Mel about the party, and that we needed to leave promptly at half past six. While I took a shower Mel got out one of my standard courtroom outfits for me; a suit and tie in muted charcoals, and a powder blue shirt. Mel came out of the bedroom an hour later wearing a top and skirt in shades of blue. I thought we looked quite chic.

We picked up Mrs. Jennings twenty minutes later. Dressed in a dark pantsuit with her hair tied up in a French twist, she looked like a no-nonsense professional woman, except that her makeup looked a little too vivid.

The most direct route from Mrs. Jennings' house to Struthers' place took us through Cornell University into the picturesque village of Cayuga Heights. Because its streets had originally been cow paths, they were a labyrinth of twisting roads extending north from the university along East Hill, rarely intersecting at right angles.

Along the border between Cornell's campus and Cayuga Heights we passed some of the most imposing homes in the area. Although most of them had been converted into sororities and fraternities, a few of them were still private residences. Some of the people living in Cayuga Heights did so for prestige.

Some of them were so wealthy they didn't care about prestige. Some were wannabes who could only afford to live there by running up ruinous debts.

I found Struthers' place on my second pass thorough the jumble of village streets. Actually I found his house number displayed prominently on a cut-stone, arched entry two stories tall. A cluster of brick chimneys was visible in the distance above the ten-foot-high stone wall enclosing the property.

As I pulled through a set of ornate iron gates onto a freshly surfaced driveway wide enough for two cars to pass easily, a castle appeared before us, well what passes for a medieval castle in Upstate New York. The two story stone pile spread out to the left and right of the central feature, which was the requisite crenelated tower. It was an impressive show of affluence, not so much an accurate representation of a medieval structure.

Mrs. Jennings asked me whose place it was. I watched for her reaction in my rearview mirror. She stiffened visibly when I told her.

"I wouldn't have come if I'd known, she said."

"The best time to slay a dragon is when it's asleep in its lair. No one here is expecting us; all the dragons are asleep."

We were greeted inside the gates by a young man who directed us to an imaginary parking place on a large manicured lawn. I worried about how things would go when I didn't see Mike's, car, but there wouldn't be another chance to get everybody in one place, so it was now never.

The temperature, unusually warm for an early October evening, would drop precipitously when the sun set on the cloudless sky. Two serving girls, wearing black and white maid uniforms, complete with short puffy skirts and black stockings, milled about among the arriving guests. Each of them carried a tray with a dozen or more wine flutes, the liquids in them turned fiery red or a soft golden hue by the late day sun. In my world, that kind of service only existed in shallow romantic novels and little girls' imaginations. I passed on the wine until I could eat some carbohydrates. Mrs. Jennings and Mel each took a glass.

On the way to the house, two other waitresses met us with trays of hors d'oeuvres. I held a hand up, declining the first girl's offer of crackers spread with a pâté I didn't recognize. The other girl carried a tray of jumbo shrimp arranged in a ring around a bowl of cocktail sauce. I grabbed one of the shrimp. Mel made a disparaging face after eating one of the crackers.

The fieldstone house, complete with a crenelated three story tower, was probably built early in the twentieth century. Easily three times the size of our place, it looked as though it had been transplanted from eighteenth century Ireland. Melodic strains of a selection from Vivaldi's *Four Seasons* emanated from the house. A horse-drawn carriage, complete with uniformed driver and footman, was parked beside the driveway. I asked the driver if he was for hire, thinking it might be something fun to do later with Mel.

"Oh no, sir, there's no charge," he said, respectfully, although I got the feeling he considered me a rube. "Mr. Struthers hired the carriage for the enjoyment of his guests." He asked if we'd like to go for a ride. I told him we might take him up on it later.

The path leading to the front door had been constructed of slate slabs the size of picnic tables. A uniformed man bowed slightly as he opened the front door for us. Two young women standing in the entryway offered to take our coats. I asked them where we would find Struthers. When they told me we'd find him on the back lawn near the barbeque pit, we decided to keep our coats. Being locals, we knew the temperature would plummet soon.

Before leaving to find him, I stepped into the adjoining room where a small chamber orchestra had just finished playing the Vivaldi piece and had started a selection from Copland's *Appalachian Spring*. I'd never heard that piece played live, and they sounded superb, so I stayed to listen. It gave Mel and Mrs. Jennings a chance to stand still and drink their wine.

If it had been my place and I was serving red wine, I would have covered the expensive-looking white carpet with plastic drop cloths, but then I have a lot less class and even less money. After a while a young man came and took the empty wine glasses from Mel and Mrs. Jennings.

Even in the house we could smell food cooking. I followed my nose through the house to a set of doors that opened onto to a huge expanse of lawn overlooking Cayuga Lake; a lawn so crowded with guests that making our way through them required both patience and courtesy.

The sound of crackling animal fat drew me to a motorized rotisserie grill filled with sizzling meats. It had been mounted over a stone-lined cooking pit, probably twelve feet long, filled with charcoal and aromatic wood chips. I'd never seen a privately-owned, custom-made, barbeque pit. No doubt he'd had it put in just for the party.

Dozens of veggie kabobs were warming on a raised shelf along the back edge of the pit. More uniformed young people stood next to tables arranged in a semi-circle around the cooking pit, poised to serve a variety of side dishes, salads, and desserts.

I checked out the crowd, wondering which one of them was Struthers, while Mel made disparaging remarks about the pit. "Somewhere out there is a herd of cattle with no ribs, and they'll probably put chicken and shrimp on the endangered species list after tonight."

"So, Mel, I've often wondered. Wealthy people often go to parties where they serve mountains of delicious food. And yet so many of them look fit and trim."

"Their vastly superior genetic makeup compels them to eat vegetables even when their senses are assaulted by the sound and aroma of grilling fat."

I asked one of the kids serving food which one of the men was S0truthers. He pointed to a group of well-groomed, middle-aged men standing apart from the main crowd. He told me Struthers was the one doing the talking.

I recognized several of the men in the group as local politicians and spotted Francis among them with Ginger hanging on his arm. Her magnificent figure was obscured by loose-fitting tan slacks and a fluffy white waist-jacket. And her makeup looked professionally done. Ginger could look classy when he wanted to, classy enough to give Francis bragging rights. She knew how to play to her audience. I had been looking forward to seeing the guest's reactions when he showed up with the Ginger I knew.

Of the men courting Struthers' favor that day, most of them picked at their food, although one overweight fellow was consuming his food with enthusiasm, and two especially-well-groomed men were drinking their dinner from crystal whiskey glasses.

We meandered through the crowd trying not to bump into anyone holding a plate of food. When I heard a commotion behind us and turned around to check, I spotted Arthur standing just outside the back door scanning the crowd. He backhanded a young man who looked like some kind of hired security. The man staggered backwards. I couldn't believe Eams was strong enough to do that, until I saw the gun he was holding.

Looking as though he'd just gotten up from a nap and hadn't bothered to comb his hair or straighten out his clothes, Arthur headed toward the crowd milling around Struthers. Unfortunately, without Mike there, it was up to me to me to prevent Arthur from doing something stupid. I told Mrs. Jennings to follow me then headed off on a course that ensured I would collide with him before he confronted Struthers. Start from here

I stopped in Arthur's path, but Arthur, with his full attention focused on Struthers, veered off to go around me without recognizing me. He raised the gun and pointed at Struthers but didn't have a clear shot. I stepped in front of him, saying, "Arthur," as loudly and forcefully as I dared, not wanting to alarm the people standing nearby; most of whom hadn't seen the gun yet.

Arthur scowled at me, mumbling something unintelligible. Then I saw the recognition dawning, confusion replacing the anger. "What are you doing here, Andy?"

Taking Mrs. Jennings by the elbow I gently pulled her forward, next to me. Her presence startled him. "Candy?"

He'd done well to recognize her after sixteen years of changes. Then he looked at each of us in turn, as though he'd just seen us for the first time. The hand holding the gun dropped to his side. Nodding at Mrs. Jennings, he asked me, "What's she doing here?"

I told him to put the gun away. He looked down at his hand. The gun seemed to surprise him. He slipped it into the pocket of his pants. I heard Mike's voice then. Because he was dressed casually in light brown chinos and a white cotton shirt with pink stripes, I assumed that he'd come right from work. Looking us over then frowning, he said, "You guys aren't eating?"

I told him we both ate before we left so it wouldn't interfere with my plans.

"Well I haven't had lunch or dinner, and smelling all that barbecued meat on an empty stomach would be the cruelest of tortures. So give me time to fill a plate before you start the fireworks." "Besides," he said, before walking away, "Struthers is buying. When will I get another chance to eat on his dime?"

I yelled after him, "I'm fine, Mike, thanks for asking," but he was already stalking the BBQ pit like a predator.

Mike joined us a few minutes later carrying a plastic dinner plate piled so high with food I thought it would fail. The cup of steaming coffee in his other hand meant he didn't have a free hand to eat with.

When he looked at my hands I knew what was coming. "Hold my coffee, Andy." With a hand free to hold his fork, he began shoveling food into his mouth as though he was stoking a boiler.

I asked him if he was going to eat the mountain of food on his plate.

Mike waved his fork in a grand sweeping gesture that encompassed Struthers' entire property. "'Crime doesn't pay' is a curious old adage, isn't it?"

"You are so right," Mel said. "Just think of all the sins it took to pay for this."

Mike stopped shoveling food and frowned thoughtfully. "There's no way a few drug-addicted naked women can generate this kind of money by gyrating to oldies in a foul-smelling dive. So it must be the drugs paying for this."

"Or maybe it's a show of money he doesn't have. I mean, just because I drive a Mercedes, that doesn't mean I have money."

Mike stopped mid-forkful. "Since when do you drive a Mercedes, Andy?"

I told him I was speaking rhetorically.

"Yeah sure, I knew that."

I asked him if he'd listened to the ensemble inside. He shook his head.

"If you get a chance, you should. They're really quite good. And it probably cost Struthers what I make in a month just to hire them for the evening."

He told me he had better things to do with his time then went back to work on his dinner. A few minutes later he stopped abruptly, with a forkful of potato salad inches from his mouth. "Hey," he said, "I see your buddy Eams is already here."

I told Mike that Arthur wasn't my buddy. I didn't tell him that Arthur had pulled a gun on Struthers.

The potato salad finally made it to his mouth. He chewed it slowly, Maybe the half plate of food he'd already consumed had taken the edge off his hunger. Then the hand holding his fork fell to his side. Something had caught his eye. "Andy, you have got to check out the good-looking young woman with Francis."

"Her name is Ginger. She's a dancer at the Tender Loin."

"Francis must be paying her because nobody who looks that good would be with him for any other reason."

I poked Mike gently with my elbow so I wouldn't spill his food. "Let's go find Struthers and get this show started, shall we? I asked Arthur and Mrs, Jennings to come with us."

As he walked with us, Mike went back to work on the remnants of his dinner. "Damn it, Andy," he said, "my food got cold," but he picked at it anyway.

Ginger was standing next to Francis, who was working on a plateful of spareribs, the sauce posing a serious threat to her fluffy white coat. I led Mike and Mel over to talk with her. On the way Mike said he'd add accessory to murder to Arthur's list of lifetime achievements.

When Francis spotted us, he pointed at me and asked Mike, "What are you doing here with him?"

"We have a few questions for our esteemed host, Mr. Struthers."

"That mistake will cost you dearly, Mike."

I told Francis he was no longer relevant and asked Ginger to come with us, which she did.

Francis yelled after us, "You haven't heard the end of this, Andrew, and neither have you, Mike."

The four of us walked over to the group of men clustered around Struthers. Mike forced his way in among them. When Struthers noticed Mike his narrative ended mid-sentence and mid-gesture, his expression morphing from confidence to confusion to anger. When he saw Ginger, he seemed genuinely surprised, no doubt surprised to see her there, not to mention surprised at how much better she looked than she ever had at the Tender Loin. He pointed a finger at her. "You of all people, don't belong here."

I told her to stay. She stood behind Mike and me.

Then Struthers' directed his anger at Mike. "You can't just waltz in here and upset my guests."

"Actually, Struthers, I can."

The men who'd been listening so attentively to Struthers backed away from him, but didn't leave. Mike glanced around at them, told Struthers', "I wouldn't worry too much about upsetting this bunch. Most of them are in my mugshot version of who's who. And as for disrupting your party, I'm investigating a murder, and you know as well as I do, it's a felony to interfere with a murder investigation."

Struthers told one of the men standing near him to go get

Francis. Then he told Ginger, "If you can't keep your trap shut, I'll have someone shut it for you."

I noticed Mike grin slightly before telling Ginger. "If he or any of his goons lay so much as a finger on you, they'll be spending the night at cell block central."

Struthers blurted out, "She's an addict and a whore. You can't believe anything she says."

Mike waved to two uniformed policemen. Most of the men in the group around us left when they saw the uniforms coming. Mike told the officers to cuff Struthers. Struthers looked angry enough to chew broken glass.

One of the policemen looked surprised, asked, "Take him to the station?"

"No," Mike said, "leave him here. I'll keep an eye on him. But go find Jack and cuff him then bring him here."

Over the buzz of dozens of conversations, I heard melodic strains coming from inside, meat sizzling on the grill, and gulls cawing as they circled overhead. A breeze blew the smell of crackling fat my way, an intense temptation. By then our group consisted of myself, Mike, Mel, Ginger, Mrs. Jennings, and Arthur.

Before everyone had settled down, Mike announced, "Okay Andy, this is your show. Go ahead. Get it started."

"There's two threads running through this mess. There's what actually happened sixteen years ago, and what Dean had planned. To understand the recent events, we need to start with the murder of the prior owner of the Tender Loin."

I told Mrs. Jennings that she was up first. "During Dean's trial sixteen years ago, you testified that Dean killed Herb. But it wasn't Dean, was it?"

Mrs. Jennings shook her head.

"Then why risk jail time by testifying that it was?"

"I wanted out of the business, Mr Lee, and I needed to get away from Dean."

"I think there must be more to it than that, or you would have been okay with some cash and a bus ticket. So what aren't

171

you telling us?"

She shook her head again.

Mike stepped in to give her a nudge. "You may not have been complicit in the actual murder, but you were in on the cover up, and that makes you an accessory to murder, and there's no statute of limitations on murder, Mrs. Jennings. You can still go to jail for it, or you can tell us the whole truth."

I asked her what would happen to Sara if she went to jail."

"Okay, I'll tell you, but under one condition. No one can know that Dean is Sara's father."

I saw that as a problem. "But Dean will know. Won't he say something?"

"Why would he? How would being a father benefit him?"

I could see Mike mulling things over. I suspect he was weighing the merits of retrying the old case. "We can't stop Dean from saying anything, but your secret is safe with me."

"How about you Mr. Lee?"

"If it's okay with Mike, It's okay with me."

"Arthur?"

Arthur shrugged his shoulders. "It's nothing to me."

"Then I'll tell you what happened. A couple of days before the murder I told Struthers I was pregnant and that Dean was the father. He said he'd pay for an abortion. He didn't want to lose a money making dancer. I told him I wanted to have the child but I didn't want Dean to know about it, and that I didn't want Dean anywhere near the child. He wouldn't agree to it. So I threatened to go to the police and tell them about the drugs and about Dean molesting the girls at the club. He got hopping mad. I think he would've done some damage to me, but I would still be a good money maker until I started showing. He told me he'd let me know what he decided. And just between us, I'll bet he was angry at Dean for getting me pregnant."

"Desperate or not, Mike said, when she took a pause, "that still took guts."

"Okay, Mrs. Jennings," I said, "take us to the trial."

"Arthur came to me after the murder. He said Struthers

would set me up with a place to live and give me a stipend to hold me over until the baby was born and I found a job. I asked him what I had to do for it. He told me I had to continue dancing until I was showing. And I had to tell the police that Dean killed Herb, and I had to testify against him if they asked me to. Considering the mess I was in, can you blame me for agreeing?"

I nodded to Mrs. Jennings as a signal that she could stop because I wanted to jump ahead to some of the recent events. "So now we now know Mrs. Jennings role in what happened sixteen years ago, and we know that her testimony got Dean convicted and sent to prison. Remember that Dean watched her testify, so a lot of his anger was directed at her.

"Just forward to last week and Dean's plans for revenge. He kidnapped Sara to use as leverage against Mrs. Jennings. That why he showed her Sara's purse."

"I'm sorry, Mrs, Jennings, I know this will be tough for you, but please tell us what Dean told you. We don't need to know what happened, just what he told you."

"He said if I wanted Sara back unharmed, I had to do what he told me to do. And if I ever said anything to anyone about what happened to either of us that night, he'd come for Sara."

I thanked Mrs. Jennings then led Mike a few feet away so she wouldn't hear me tell him, "Dean's revenge against Mrs. Jennings wasn't just sex that she'd regret for the rest of her life. It was also worrying about what he could still do to Sara at some later date if Mrs. Jennings ever told anyone what had happened that night."

I saw the uniforms bringing Jack to us then. Good timing, because I had a question for him, "Whatever transpired between Dean and Mrs. Jennings, when it was done, Dean called Jack and told him to drop Sara off at her mother's ASAP. He was counting on Sara being returned quickly and without a scratch, so Mrs. Jennings wouldn't go to the police."

With Mike in tow, I returned to the group to ask Mrs. Jennings a question. "Mrs. Jennings, would you have gone to the police if Sara had been returned unharmed?"

She shook her head. "Not if Sara had been okay."

Mike asked, "Is there a point to this, Andy?"

"The point is, that except for the kidnapping, Dean is innocent of the charges against him. He's been framed just like he was sixteen years ago."

"I don't suppose he has an alibi."

"In a way he does, Mike. You see, he was busy somewhere else."

"Busy where, doing what?"

"We'll get to that in just a minute. First I want to finish up with Jack. He raped Sara while Dean was with her mother."

"How do you figure that?"

"We know from Sara's statement that she was in the van for a while before Dean put her in a bed, and that she was kept there until she was brought home. Mrs. Jennings' statement said that Dean left her place just before one-fifteen. She was alerted to Sara being dropped off by the neighbor's dogs barking. The dogs also woke up the neighbor, and he happened to check his clock. He told the police that was about one-forty. That's only twenty-five minutes. But the round trip to the cabin to get Sara and take her home would have taken Dean an hour. I know. I had Rick time it."

"But Sara said that Dean was there with her the whole time."

"Jack put on some of Dean's cologne."

"That might fly, but only if Dean has an alibi."

"Remember when I said that Dean was busy doing something while Jack was taking Sara home?"

"Yeah, Andy, I remember, but get to the punchline. The suspense is killing me."

"And he was busy killing Sheila."

The look of surprise on Mike's face quickly morphed into a frown. "That leaves some gaps in the story, Andy. Please do fill us in."

I asked Ginger to repeat for Mike what she'd told me about Arthur's keys, but before she could say anything, Struthers told her, "If you can't keep your trap shut, I'll have someone shut it for you."

I noticed Mike grin slightly before telling Ginger. "Don't worry about these goons, they'll be spending the night at cell block central."

Struthers blurted out, "She's an addict and a whore. You can't believe anything she says."

Mike told Struthers to shut his trap, and Ginger to tell him about the keys.

After cautious glances at Jack and Struthers, to her credit, she did tell Mike about the keys. "The night Shelia was killed Mr. Struthers told me to hide Arthur's keys under a towel in the bathroom. Next time I went in there they were gone. I found them back under the towel a couple of hours later."

Mike frowned, asked me, "So Struthers is Sheila's killer?"

"No. it happened like this. After Dean dropped Sara off at the cabin with Jack he went to Mrs. Jennings' house. From there he went to the Tender Loin and called Jack to take Sara home. He got the keys Ginger had put under the towel in the bathroom then he drove Arthur's car to the boyfriend's house, parking it where it would be spotted so Arthur would go to prison for Sheila's death. After he killed Sheila, he took Arthur's car back to the club, replacing the keys in the bathroom."

"But why Sheila. What did Dean have against her?"

"I can explain, but it requires digging up more of the past. Arthur's going to help us with that, aren't you, Arthur?"

"No, I'm not"

The five of us stood there patiently for several moments. Mike tired of it first. "Quit stalling, Arthur."

Struthers, who was causing a commotion by struggling with the officer holding him, yelled at Arthur. "Keep your mouth shut, or you're a dead man."

Right on cue, Arthur said, "I've got nothing to say."

He had good reason to be afraid of Struthers, but even more reason to cooperate. "Arthur, if you tell us what happened, Struthers will never bother you again, because he'll be rotting in prison. Otherwise you'll be fair game."

Arthur grimaced then looked away from Struthers then started to explain. "I did the books for Herb back then and Strothers ran the day-to-day operations. One day Herb told Struthers that he'd been putting cash aside so he could buy extra drugs, in hopes of doubling sales. Struthers didn't think it was a good idea. He was afraid the police would put them out of business because of it.

"One day when I was in Herb's office going over the books with him, Struthers came in. He got into it with Herb over expanding the drug operation. After they went back and forth a few times, Herb told Struthers that he'd made up his mind, told him to arrange for an extra-large purchase. Struthers asked him how much. Herb told him to spend whatever was in the safe. From what I knew of the books, there was probably tens of thousands in there.

"Anyway, the safe was in the wall behind Herb's desk. When Struthers went to open it, Herb turned his back on him to talk to me. Struthers took a glass vase off of a shelf near the safe, one of the ones made of really thick, heavy glass. He clocked Herb with it, hit him real hard. Herb slumped down then fell out of his chair onto the floor and stayed there, deader than old road kill.

"I couldn't believe Struthers had killed him. He asked me if I wanted to help him run the place, asked if I'd stay on as his accountant. I told him I didn't want any part of it."

Struthers chose that moment to yell, "You're a dead, Eams."

It made Arthur cringe, but he went on. "After I told him I wanted out, he got real quiet; just stood there staring at me. That went on so long I thought he might come after me with the vase. But eventually he told me he'd let me out, that he'd even give me a stake, 30 thousand, if I did something for him."

He paused. I said, "That was a lot of money sixteen years ago."

"Damn right it was. But most of it wasn't for me. I was

supposed to set Candy up with a place of her own and give her a monthly stipend until she got a job. In return she had to tell the police that Dean killed Herb, and she had to testify to it if they wanted her to."

Mike asked him why Struthers didn't just handle that himself.

"Because he knew Candy and I had a thing going. He thought I'd have better luck convincing her to play along and keeping her on track."

"For you, this wasn't about the money, was it, Arthur? You had it in for Dean because he'd raped your girl, and not just once. Have I got that right?"

"Yeah, that's right."

I asked Mrs. Jennings to show Mike the scar above her ear. "That was your doing, wasn't it, Arthur?"

Mel couldn't let that go. "Jesus, Arthur, you did that to your girlfriend?"

"That was part of the deal. No scar, no money. It was a test. A way for me to prove I took the deal seriously."

Mel's red face was turning an even deeper red. "You did it for money?"

"If I hadn't, Struthers might have put her on the street with nothing but a new kid coming and no way to fend for herself."

"And you couldn't help her?"

"With what Struthers had at stake, I thought he'd kill her if she didn't cooperate."

"But why a scar?"

"He thought it would make her testimony more convincing to the police and to a jury."

"That's right," Mrs. Jennings said, "I told them Dean did it to me as a warning to keep my mouth shut."

Mike asked her, "And neither the police nor the DA questioned your story?"

"I think they wanted Dean put away as much as we did."

"Arthur," I said, "why didn't Struthers didn't just renege

and keep the thirty thousand after Candy had testified?"

"Candy and I could've ruined him if we'd gone to the police with the truth. I think he might have killed one of us, but hiding two more killings was more than he wanted to risk."

So Mrs. Jennings had been paid handsomely for her participation in the plot. That wouldn't sit well with a jury, if it ever came to that. I hoped it wouldn't, in spite of my desire for justice.

"Forgive me," I said, "but I feel the need to recap some of what happened. First, Candy told Struthers she was pregnant, which meant he'd have to find a replacement. Then after killing Herb, Struthers needed to find a scapegoat. And when Arthur refused to join him running the business, he had another problem; how to keep Arthur from talking. Last but not least, he didn't want Dean around causing trouble while he was running the business. Framing Dean for the murder solved all of that."

"Yeah, okay," Mike said, "but how does all of this fit with Dean's confession?"

"He signed it right after I talked to Mrs. Jennings. He thought she might tell me something that would expose his connections to Arthur and Struthers?"

"He signed the confession so you'd stop digging."

"That and he knew rape would get him from five to twenty-five years. Murder would get him twenty-five to life. Even though it was bogus, the conviction for Herb's murder made him a repeat offender, increasing the likelihood that he would get the maximum sentence."

"So," Mike said, "Dean killed Sheila, and Struthers killed Herb. But who killed Reed, and why?"

"Struthers ordered Jack and Nate to take care of him. I saw Jack's truck at the warehouse when I went to meet Reed."

"Who's Nate?"

I asked Ginger to answer him.

"Nate is Struthers' little brother. Jack uses him like a toy, makes him do the real dirty work."

Mike asked me, "But why would any of them risk going

to prison for killing Reed if he was just a witness to the kidnapping?"

"If Reed hadn't pulled Dean's mask up, Sara wouldn't have been able to make a positive ID from Dean's mug shot. That's how he was arrested so quickly. But besides that, Reed knew enough about Dean's plans to get him put away."

"What could he have known that was worth having him killed?"

"Remember that Dean called Jack and told him to take Sara home. According to Dean's original plan, Reed would have been at the cabin watching Sara, so he would have called Reed to take her home. Dean would have gone over the plan with Reed ahead of time to be sure Reed understood what was expected of him."

"Sorry, Andy, but that's not convincing."

"This is Dean we're dealing with, Mike. He might have killed Reed in a fit of rage, or because he felt like it."

"So Struthers sent Jack and Nate to kill Reed." Mike picked at the food on his plate half-heartedly for a while then said, "We'll table that while you tell me why Dean would kill Sheila instead of Arthur?"

"Believe it or not, Mike, I think Arthur actually loved Sheila, and I suspect Dean knew it."

"How would he know that?"

"The girls at the club maybe. But let's assume it's true for a minute. Knowing that would make for some very sweet revenge. Then the longer Arthur lived, the longer he'd suffer. And imagine the kind of abuse a flabby weakling like Arthur would suffer in prison. Dean knew first-hand what would befall Arthur in there, and no doubt he planned to savor it."

I could tell Mike was working his way through it, because, although he did nod his head, he was still frowning.

"And one more thing, Mike. Killing Sheila instead of Arthur made the murder harder to solve. Because, without digging up the past, there was no apparent connection between Dean and Sheila. I hate to say it, Mike, but Dean might be smarter than we thought."

"So I should charge Nate with killing Reed, and Struthers and Jack as accessories. I should charge Dean with killing Sheila, and Struthers as an accessory. I should charge Jack for raping Sara. And the charges against Dean for kidnapping Sara and raping her mother should stand. Have I got all of that right?"

"You do."

"I will enjoy seeing Jack behind bars most of all. Hell, I may go see him just to gloat."

"Can't blame you there, Mike."

"Humor me, Andy, while I recap some of this. Arthur and Jennings kept silent because they were accessories to the murder sixteen years ago. And Jennings didn't want Sara to find out about her mother's sordid past or who her real father was. Dean knew it was Jack who molested Sara but wouldn't finger him for it, because Jack could finger him for Sheila's murder."

"That about sums it up."

"Do you have any idea what this is gonna do to my paperwork?" Mike frowned at the food on his plate then walked over to a row of garbage cans on the edge of the lawn that were camouflaged with bunting and tossed his plate in.

When he rejoined us he said, "Feeling smug, are we, Andy?"

"Why would you say that?"

"You proved that both of your clients were innocent of the original charges, but still managed to reserve rooms for them on felony row. And thanks to you, Struthers, Jack, and Nate will be in there with them. But do me a favor. Next time, don't leave me in the dark until the last minute. It makes me look bad."

"Sorry Mike, but the last time Mel and I stopped by your office, I didn't feel welcome."

"Tell you what, Andy, I'll forget the trespassing charge if you'll tell me how you unraveled this mess."

"When I began to suspect that everything was tied to the past, I got serious about digging it up. It was like putting a jigsaw puzzle together without the picture. You don't know you've put in enough pieces until, like magic, the image appears. Then you wonder why you hadn't seen it before."

Mike left us then to go with the officers taking Jack and Struthers away. The mild evening air was dominated by an irresistible smorgasbord of aromas coming from the assortment of fats still sizzling in the barbecue pit, but with the host being led away in cuffs, there would soon be a crush of people trying to get their cars out through the front gates. If we left immediately we might beat the rush.

I told Ginger we'd give her a ride then looked for a way to get to the front yard without going through the house. I didn't want to walk past Nate with Ginger in tow. Unfortunately, all of the exits from the back yard were blocked, no doubt to discourage uninvited guests.

I stopped at the door to hold it open for Mel, and Ginger, and Mrs. Jennings. Ginger went through first. I heard a commotion erupt almost immediately.

I went in next to check. People had backed away, giving me a clear view of the room. Nate was holding Ginger securely from behind. He held a knife at her throat.

When he saw me he asked where his brother was. "I'll take you to him, Nate, but you have to let her go first."

He became more agitated. The knife was tight against Ginger's neck, tight enough that a sudden motion could draw blood or worse.

It's the only way you'll get to see him, Nate."

We faced each other for what seemed an interminable time before he shoved Ginger away. I approached him. He held the knife out threateningly. I gestured toward the front door, hoping he'd lead the way. I didn't want him behind me. The crowd parted for him. I followed.

What little plan I had started with getting him out of there, away from Mel and Ginger. The rest of it consisted of driving him to the police station under the pretense of seeing his brother, and hoping I could think of a better plan before the police station came into view. I had no doubt Nate would go berserk if he saw it.

Nate suddenly lurched to the right. I turned left away from his knife. Mike had him; wrestled with him. The knife fell. Mike got Nate in a half Nelson. Nate struggled, but it was pointless. I went back to find the women while Mike took Nate away. When we got to the front yard, Nate was in cuffs in the back seat of Mike's car.

Mike, who was leaning on the car, said, "What the hell were you thinking, Andy?"

"Lucky for me you were still here."

Lucky for you I had that big coffee with my dinner. I had to go back inside to pee before I left for the station."

So you're saying I owe my life to your bladder?"

"It would seem so. And by the way, Andy, nice job figuring all this out."

An hour later, having dropped off Mrs. Jennings and Ginger, Mel and I were sitting on a squeaky swinging bench on the shore of Cayuga Lake at Stewart Park. Snuggled under a blanket we keep in the car, we watched the first of the evening stars sparkling overhead and listened to the rhythmic lap of the waves.

"Mike's right," Mel said, "The way you sorted this mess out in spite of all the lies was impressive. I just wish Sara had been dealt a better hand."

"Really, Mel, a metaphor?"

"I hate to say it, Andy, but it looks like your stubbornness paid off."

"I prefer to think of it as tenacity, Mel"

"And you cleared the board of all the bad players."

"Another metaphor? What got into you?"

She smiled. "Let's just hope that all the evil stirred up sixteen years ago has finally been put to rest."

The conversation ended there. The familiar scent of her hair was pleasant and reassuring in an unsettled world. We had our lives back. The next chapter was ours to write, but it would keep until tomorrow.